Perfect Little Children

SOPHIE HANNAH

Perfect
Little Children

WM

WILLIAM MORROW
An Imprint of HarperCollins*Publishers*

PERFECT LITTLE CHILDREN. Copyright © 2020 by Sophie Hannah.
All rights reserved. Printed in the United States of America. No part of this book
may be used or reproduced in any manner whatsoever without written permission
except in the case of brief quotations embodied in critical articles and reviews.
For information, address HarperCollins Publishers,
195 Broadway, New York, NY 10007.

HarperCollins books may be purchased for educational, business, or sales
promotional use. For information, please email the Special Markets Department
at SPsales@harpercollins.com.

Originally published as *Haven't They Grown* in the United Kingdom
in January 2020 by Hodder & Stoughton.

FIRST U.S. EDITION

Library of Congress Cataloging-in-Publication Data has been applied for.

ISBN 978-0-06-297820-2 (hardcover)
ISBN 978-0-06-298850-8 (international edition)

20 21 22 23 24   LSC   10 9 8 7 6 5 4 3 2 1

For Dan, Phoebe, Guy and Brewstie

1

April 20, 2019

Here we are, in the wrong place: Wyddial Lane. It's a private road, as the sign unsubtly proclaims in letters larger than those spelling out its name, in a village called Hemingford Abbots. I switch off the engine, stretch my back to release the ache from two hours of driving, and wait for Ben to notice that there's no football ground in sight.

He's buried in his phone. I can't help thinking of it like that—as if he's stuck inside the machine in his hand, unable to get out. Quite happy about it, too. Zannah's the same. Most teenagers are, as far as I can tell: they spend all day and half the night in lock-eyed communion with an addictive device. No amount of my children telling me it's "the way life is these days, so stop being so old and just chill" will ever persuade me to think it's okay. It's not. It's frightening and depressing.

Sometimes it's also useful, to a parent who doesn't want to be scrutinized. It's likely to be a while before Ben notices the intense quiet—almost total silence, apart from the occasional bird chirp or gust of wind rustling the branches of the trees that line Wyddial Lane on both sides—and realizes that there are no teenage boys in football shirts traipsing past our car or anywhere nearby. He's completely immersed: head down, lips moving as he types with his thumbs. I've probably got two minutes at least.

Plenty of time. You can take in a lot in a hundred and twenty seconds, and that's all I came here to do: have a good look. Many times over the past twelve years, I've wondered about

Flora's new house. Technically it ceased to be "new" at least a decade ago, though that's still how I think of it. I checked last year to see if the "Street View not available in this location" message still came up, and it did. Maybe that's got something to do with it being a private road. I can't think what else it would be. Until today, I assumed that Wyddial Lane was very remote, but it isn't. Despite the peaceful rural vibe, it's only two minutes from a main road.

I've no idea what kind of house I'd buy if, suddenly, money were no object, and I've always been curious to see what Flora and Lewis chose—certainly not curious enough to devote half a day to the four-hour round trip, especially when I might be spotted on my spying mission and I'd have no way to explain my presence, but interested enough to recognize a perfect opportunity when one presented itself. As soon as the list of impending football fixtures arrived and I saw "St. Ives, Cambridgeshire," I knew what I was going to do. It felt like a reward for all those Saturdays spent driving Ben around, all the hours I've stood shivering by the sides of muddy fields far from home while he played. Finally a perk had been handed to me and I resolved on the spot to take full advantage of it.

Today, if by any chance Flora or Lewis catches sight of me here, my excuse will be so close to the truth that it might as well be the truth: I'm driving my son to his Regional League match nearby and I took a wrong turn. Ben, sitting beside me in his red and white football gear, would be all the proof I'd need. Only the "wrong turn" part of the story would be false.

For a better view, I've parked across the road from number 16, not directly outside it. To the left of the thick wooden gates, there's a square sign, gray stone, attached to the high brick wall that protects all but the very top of the house from prying eyes like mine. The sign says, "Newnham House."

I shake my head. Unbelievable, that they chose to call it that.

And those gates, a foot higher at their uppermost point than the top of the wall . . . Most of the houses here have high walls surrounding them. Being on a private road doesn't offer these people enough privacy, apparently.

Of course the home of The New Flora and Lewis Braid looks like this. I should have been able to predict it all: the ugly, sprawling modern mansion, the private road, the gates kidding themselves that they don't appear superior and unfriendly because they've got curly flourishes at the top that look marginally more welcoming than the seven feet of dense wood immediately beneath them.

There's a silver box with buttons below the "Newnham House" sign—an intercom. I'd need to press those buttons if I wanted to gain access, which I definitely don't.

Is this what too much money does to people? Or is it only what too much money does to Lewis Braid? There's no way this house is Flora's choice—not the Flora I knew. And Lewis had a knack for getting his way whenever they disagreed.

"Where are we? This isn't the ground." My son has finally noticed his surroundings.

"I know."

"Then why've we stopped? I thought you knew where we're going?"

"I do."

"The warm-up starts in, like, fifteen minutes."

"And it'll only take us ten to drive there. Lucky, eh?" I smile brightly, switching on the engine.

Ben turns back to his phone with a sigh. He is considerate enough not to say, "I wish Dad was driving me." According to our family folklore, Dominic is a good driver who plans well and allows enough time, and I am the opposite. This week was Dom's turn to do football duty. He couldn't believe his luck when I said I fancied an outing and offered to go instead. I doubt he remembers that Flora and Lewis moved to very near St. Ives soon after we last saw them. Even if he does, he wouldn't suspect I had a secret agenda. Dominic would never take a ten-minute detour in order to see the current home of someone he hadn't seen for twelve years—therefore, in his mind, neither would I.

"Fuck off!" Ben says to his phone.

"Ben. What have we—"

"Sorry." He makes that sound like a swear word too. "Do you have a list of everything Dad's ever done wrong?"

"What? No, of course not."

"So it's not normal, then? Most people in relationships don't do it?"

"A written list? Definitely not."

"Lauren's got a list on her phone of everything I've done wrong since we've been a thing."

Lauren, a model-level-beautiful girl who is excessively polite to me and eats nothing apart from noodles according to both my children, describes herself as Ben's girlfriend. He objects to this terminology and insists that they are merely "a thing."

"But you've never done anything wrong to Lauren, have you? Or have you?" They've only been together—if that's the right way to put it—for three weeks.

"I put two 'x's in my last message instead of three. That's the latest thing."

"Did you do it deliberately?"

"No. I didn't even know I'd done it. Didn't think about it."

I indicate to turn onto the main road, wishing I had a choice and could stay a bit longer on Wyddial Lane. Why? I did what I wanted to do, saw what there was to see from the outside. That ought to feel like enough.

"Who the fu— Who *counts kisses* in a message?" Ben says.

"Girls do. Some girls, anyway. Lauren's obviously one of them."

"First the problem was me not doing it—she'd always put a line of 'x's at the bottom of her messages and I never would, and she thought that meant I don't care about her—so I started putting them in, and now she's counting how many, and thinking it *means* something if I do one less than in the last message. That's crazy, right?"

"Ask Zannah if she counts how many kisses Murad puts in each message." Murad, to my knowledge, has only once done something wrong in the year and a half that he and Zannah have been whatever-they-call-it, and he turned up looking tearful the following morning, clutching a dozen red roses. Zannah was delighted, both by the roses and by the news of the sleepless night he'd suffered after "criticizing me when I'd done fuck all wrong. Mum, I literally don't care what you think about me swearing right now. Sometimes I *need* to swear, or I'd throw myself off a bridge."

I would be very surprised if my daughter did not keep on top of the kisses-per-message statistics.

Ben groans. "And now, because I didn't instantly reply and say 'Oh, sorry, sorry,' and send a long line of 'x's, she's going to accuse me of blanking her."

"So why not reply and send more kisses?"

"No! Why should I?"

"You're right. You shouldn't." Poor boy. He's fourteen, for God's sake—too young to be engaged in fraught relationship negotiations.

"I've done nothing wrong. Ask Zannah, Mum. Lauren's a high-maintenance, needy—"

"Ben!"

"*Person*. I was going to say 'person.'"

"Yeah. Course you were." I'm glad his instinct is to stand up for himself, and that he's not planning to cry all night and take roses around to Lauren's house tomorrow morning.

Ten minutes later we're parked in the right place. Ben climbs out of the car. "You coming to watch?" he asks, tossing his phone onto the passenger seat. I usually do. I'm not remotely interested in football, but I love to see Ben doing something healthy and worthwhile, something other than being the slave of an electronic device.

"In a bit," I say. "First I want to find a supermarket and get something for dinner tonight."

I watch him run off. Soon he and other red-and-white-clad boys are pushing each other around happily—trying to trip each other up, grabbing each other's backpacks.

On the passenger seat, Ben's phone starts to ring. "Zannah" flashes up on the screen. I pick it up. "Hi, darling. Everything okay?" Zannah isn't normally awake before noon on a Saturday.

"Where's Ben?" The clipped precision of her words doesn't bode well.

"Football."

"Really? According to Snap Maps, he was on a street called Widdle Lane or something ten minutes ago. What the hell was he doing there?"

"Wyddial Lane. Yeah, that's nearby. Now we're at football."

"Right. When you next see him, can you please ask him to deal with his high-maintenance nightmare of a girlfriend? Thanks. She's just called me and *woken me up* to tell me that Ben blanked her in the middle of an important conversation, and can I ask him to message her? Their pathetic relationship is not my problem, Mum, and I'm not getting dragged into it."

"I—"

"Thanks, Mum. See you later. I'm going back to sleep. Ugh, it's *nine thirty*—grim."

She's gone. "Girlfriend," she said. So using that word in a teenage context is not entirely disallowed. I add this important clue to my ongoing study of teenage behavior, glad that my investigative interest in every aspect of my children's lives is not reciprocated. Zannah and Ben aren't remotely concerned about the details of my day-to-day life. Neither of them asked me why I drove to Wyddial Lane before going to the St. Ives football ground; neither of them ever will.

There's something comforting about living with two people who never think about or question your behavior. I tried to explain this to Dominic once, when he complained that the kids never ask how our days have been. "They're teenagers," I said. "Anything happening outside of the teenage arena, they couldn't care less. Be thankful—remember the time Ben found cigarettes and a lighter in your jacket pocket, and you told him you gave up ages ago, and they must have been there for at least ten years? You didn't mind then that he didn't pounce on that and say, 'But wait, you only bought that jacket last month.'"

I don't have any bad habits that I'm concealing from the children. I've only ever had one near miss on a par with Dominic's cigarettes-and-lighter scare, and that was when Zannah was four and still interested enough in people outside her immediate peer group to notice strange things her mother did. She walked into the kitchen and found me with a pair of scissors in one hand and a photograph in the other. I must have looked upset and guilty, because she asked me if I was okay. "Of course, darling," I said in a bright voice.

How could I have explained to a four-year-old what I was doing—or to anyone? Dominic was working in the living room, which was next to the kitchen in our old house. He'd have been horrified. I remember holding my breath, praying that my unnaturally high-pitched "Of course" hadn't aroused his suspicions. Four-year-old Zannah looked doubtful, but she didn't ask any more questions.

The photograph she'd caught me holding was of the Braid

family: Lewis and Flora and their three children—Thomas, Emily and Georgina. A happy family portrait, taken in the back garden. Flora had included it with their Christmas card. She always sent a photo, just as she always signed the card "Lewis, Flora . . ." His name had to come first because it was traditional, and the Braids cared about things like that. Dominic and I discussed it once. He said, "There's no way Lewis has ever said to Flora, 'Make sure to put my name first.' He'd totally leave the Christmas card sending to her, wouldn't he? I can't see him giving it a single second's thought."

"True," I said. "But he also would never have ended up married to the kind of woman who wouldn't automatically put his name first on all correspondence."

So often over the past twelve years, I've wanted to tell Dominic what I did to that photograph and ask him which he thinks is worse: that, or what Flora did to me.

If I did, he'd probably laugh and say, "You're mad, Beth," in an affectionate way. He'd say the same—that I must be insane—about what I'm going to do next, which isn't what I've just told Ben.

I'm not going to the supermarket to buy tonight's dinner.

I'm going back to Wyddial Lane.

I'm amazed by how much more I notice now that I'm alone and there's no pressure from an imminent football match to distract me: the black metal mailbox attached to a gatepost, with "16" on it in white, the burglar alarm, the row of what might be tiny security cameras or some kind of motion sensors lining the top of the house just under the gutters, like a string of paranoid fairy lights.

As I drove back here, the gray sky gave way to a hazy blue and the sun appeared. Now it's properly warm for the first time this year. Even with the window down, it's already too hot in the car. I don't want to put on the air conditioning—that would involve starting up the engine, and the last thing I need is for Flora to look out and wonder about the stationary car with its engine running.

That's funny: I'm assuming that, if anyone's home, it's going to be Flora. Twelve years ago, when I still knew the Braids, Lewis's job on Saturdays was to ferry Thomas and Emily around by car to their various hobby duties: swimming lessons, drama club, tennis coaching. Five-year-old Thomas and three-year-old Emily had an absurd number of unmissable appointments. Lewis drove them to and fro while Flora caught up on the housework. He often used to say, "When I sell my company for a trillion dollars, we'll have a fleet of chauffeurs and I'll be able to spend weekends watching telly with my feet up." In those days, he was always making jokes about how he would one day be rich. If we went to a crowded bar or café where we had to raise our voices to be heard, Lewis would announce, "When I'm rich I'll have four chefs living in the annex of my mansion—Indian, Italian, French and English—so that I don't have to put up with other people's noise in order to get great food." Flora would tut at his imaginary extravagance and say, "Lew-*is*," in the same voice she used to subdue her small children when they were making a spectacle of themselves in public.

As it turned out, Lewis didn't need to worry about selling his company in order to get rich. His hoarder-miser grandfather died and left him several million pounds that nobody in the Braid family had known the old man had. Lewis and Flora moved from a three-bedroom basement flat to 16 Wyddial Lane, which looks as if it must have at least eight bedrooms, and now perhaps Lewis has all those chefs and chauffeurs he used to joke about acquiring. Maybe he and Flora and their kids are all inside the house now, staring at their iPhones.

What age would Georgina be? Twelve, so not quite a teenager. We didn't let Zannah have a phone until she was thirteen, but her teenager behavior had definitely started by then. She was eleven the first time she raised her eyebrows and asked me why I imagined in my wildest dreams that she might want to go into town with someone wearing a carpet. (I was dressed in a beautiful woolen poncho at the time.)

I feel ashamed when I think about Georgina Braid, so I concentrate on the house instead. I got it wrong before—I glanced at it and decided it was modern, but, on closer inspection, it looks as if only the sides of it are newly built. The middle third of the building sticks out in front of the grand wings to the left and right, which are flat-fronted and have been added much more recently in what Zannah would call a "glow-up." The dark-red pantiled roof of the newest sections starts higher up than the roof of the middle part, which has two dormer windows set into it. Presumably this was once an average-sized cottage. Only just visible above the closed wooden gates is a lychgate-style roofed porch, with the same red tiles. Apart from the two roofs—house and porch—the entire frontage is gleaming white. It looks as if it might have been painted yesterday. The overall effect is of a sleek, contemporary white-cube-style house that has swallowed a lumpy old cottage and been unable to digest it.

There's a second building, long and low, standing between the house and the high wall, separating the two. Most likely it's a double or triple garage. If there's this much space at the front, there must be three times as much at the back, at least. I picture a long, striped lawn, alternating shades of lush green, and a smooth stone patio area, complete with top-of-the-range outdoor chairs and sofas: dark brown with plump cream cushions.

I wipe beads of sweat from my forehead. One open window isn't enough. How has it become so hot, suddenly? I open my door slightly, to let more air in.

Could I . . .

No. Absolutely not. I can't ring the bell and smile and say, "Hi, Flora. I was passing, and I thought I'd pop around on the off chance." Not after twelve years.

Is that why I came here, really? Not only to see the house but because I'm secretly hoping to rewrite the story?

The Braids and the Leesons were best friends. Twelve years ago, they did not have any sort of argument, nor did they exchange harsh words. The last time they saw each other, everybody smiled and laughed and kissed and hugged good-bye. They talked about getting together again very soon—maybe next week, maybe taking the kids to the summer fair on Parker's Piece. As they enthusiastically agreed to ring each other to arrange this outing, Flora Braid and Beth Leeson both knew that there would be no phone call in either direction, and no trip to the fair. Dominic Leeson and Lewis Braid did not know this, because no one had told them that the two families would never meet or speak again.

On the face of it, it makes no sense. Only Flora and I understand what happened—and I'll never know whether our understandings of it are the same. I've tried to explain to Dominic what happened from my point of view, and I suppose Flora must have told Lewis something, though perhaps not the truth . . .

This is ridiculous. I should be watching Ben play football, or finding a supermarket. I really do need to get something for dinner. Who cares where the Braids live now? I've seen everything there is to see—cream curtains at the upstairs windows, fat, square redbrick gateposts topped with large balls of gray stone, perfectly smooth and round, clashing horribly with the red brick.

I should go.

I'm about to start the car when I notice one coming up behind me: a Range Rover driving extra slowly. Wyddial Lane is a twenty-mile-an-hour zone, and this car's going at no more than ten. I'm watching it, willing it to speed up, when I notice a movement from another direction.

It's Flora's gates—they're opening.

The silver-gray Range Rover slows still further as it approaches the Braids' house. It inches forward, now almost level with my car. That's where it's heading: through the wooden gates, into the grounds of number 16. Of course: there's no way Lewis and Flora would have gates that you have to get out and open; they'd have some kind of remote-control setup.

I see glossy dark brown hair through the Range Rover's half-open window. It could well be Flora. It's bound to be.

Shit. Why did I think I could get away with this? She's going to see me.

No, she won't. No one looks at a random parked car. She'll drive in through the gates and then they'll close again, and she won't think about what's beyond her property.

I turn my face away, making sure to lean close to my open window in case there's anything to hear.

There's nothing for a few seconds. Then a crunch of tires on gravel, and the sound of the Range Rover's engine cutting out. A car door opens. Feet land on gravel and a woman's voice, halfway through a sentence as it emerges into the open air, drifts across to me: ". . . said I'm ready now. You can start. Yes. Start."

It's Flora. Unmistakably. She doesn't sound happy. She sounds . . . I don't know how to describe it. Afraid, resentful, prepared for the worst. Is something horrible about to happen?

Don't be ridiculous. You heard, what, six words?

I listen for a response but I hear nothing. Flora's probably on the phone.

I've never heard her sound like that before.

I can't not look. I have to risk it. If the worst happens and she spots me and I decide I can't face talking to her, I can just drive away, fast. That'd give her twenty-mile-an-hour-zone neighbors something to talk about. They could lobby to have Wyddial Lane sealed at both ends so that no one who doesn't live here can enter in future.

The gates of Newnham House are still wide open. And there's Flora: twelve years older, but it's definitely her. Her hair hasn't changed a bit: same dark brown with no hint of gray, same style. She's wearing white lace-up pumps, a pale gray hoodie and jeans.

"Home," she says, holding her phone half an inch away from her ear. "I'm at home."

I tried to push it away but it's back again: the strong sense that what I'm seeing isn't an ordinary conversation. There's something wrong.

A short silence follows. Then she says, "Hey, Chimp." She stops, raises her voice slightly and says, "Hey, Chimpyyy!"

Strange. The words don't match the expression on her face at all. She looks upset and worried, not in relaxed-greeting mode.

Is she talking to a new person now? Did the person she told she was ready put a child on the phone? It must be a child, surely. Who else would allow themselves to be called Chimpy? Her change of tone, too, from normal to deliberate, slower, louder . . .

Suddenly, she turns away and stretches out her arm, holding her phone as far away from herself as possible. Then, a few seconds later, she brings it back to her ear and wipes her eyes with her other hand.

She started to cry and didn't want Chimpy to hear.

"Peterborough," she says in a more normal tone of voice. "Lucky. I'm very lucky."

Tears have filled my eyes. I can't blink. They'd spill over

and then I'd be officially crying, which would be insane. This woman has been no part of my life for twelve years. Why should I care that something about this phone conversation has upset her?

"Yes. Tomorrow," she says. "I'll speak to you tomorrow." I watch as she puts her phone back in her bag. For a few seconds she stands still, looking tired and defeated, relieved that the conversation is over.

She opens the back door of the Range Rover, sticks her head in and says, "We're he-ere!" The deliberate jolly tone is unconvincing. Then she stands back. Nothing happens.

No surprises there. When the destination they've arrived at is their own home, teenagers don't get out of the car unless nagged extensively. If you're dropping them at a friend's house, it's a different story.

I hear Flora sigh. "Thomas! Emily!" she says in a singsong voice. "Come on, out you get!"

"Why are you speaking to them like they're still toddlers?" I mutter. "No wonder they're ignoring you."

Even when her kids were little, Flora's speaking-to-babies-and-children tone annoyed me. Thanks to her, I made sure I always addressed Zannah and Ben as if they were proper people.

Flora stands back as if someone's about to get out of the car. "That's it!" she says encouragingly.

Quit it, woman, unless you want them to run off and join a cult. They ought to be able to get out of a car without a pep talk from their mother.

A small, bright blue backpack tumbles from the car to the ground. I see a leg emerge, then a boy.

A very young boy.

What the hell?

"Come on, Emily," says Flora. "Thomas, pick up your bag."

A little girl rolls out of the car. She picks up the blue bag and hands it to the boy.

"Oh, well done, Emily," says Flora. "That's kind. Say thank you, Thomas."

This cannot be happening.

I touch the skin of my face with my right hand. Both feel equally cold. All of me feels frozen apart from my heart, which beats in my ears like something trapped in a tunnel.

I lean back in my seat, close my eyes for a few seconds, then open them and look again.

Nothing has changed. The little girl turns and, for a second, looks straight at me.

It's her. That T-shirt with the fluffy sheep on it . . . *Le petit mouton.*

The girl I'm looking at is Emily Braid, except she's not fifteen, as she should be—as she *must* be and is, unless the world has stopped making sense altogether.

This is the Emily Braid I knew twelve years ago, when she was three years old. And Thomas . . . I can't see all of his face, but I can see enough to know that he's still five years old, as he was when I last saw him in 2007.

I have to get out of here. I can't look anymore. Everything is wrong.

My fingers fumble for the car keys. I press them hard, then realize I'm pressing the wrong thing. It's the button on the dashboard, not the keys. I'm waiting for the engine to start and it won't because I'm not doing it right, because all I can think about is Thomas and Emily Braid.

Why are they—how *can* they be—still three and five? Why are they no older than they were twelve years ago?

Why haven't they grown?

2

Several hours later, walking back through my front door and closing it against the world feels like an achievement.

I made it. Me and Ben, safely home. How I was able to concentrate on driving properly, I've no idea. I probably shouldn't have risked it.

I lean against the wall in the hall, shut my eyes and let the sound of Ben telling Dominic about the match wash over me. His voice broke a few months ago, and we're still getting used to this new deeper one. His music teacher described him as a "bass" the other day, and it gave me a strange, dislocated feeling. My sweet little boy, a bass—the lowest and most booming kind of male voice there is. How did that happen?

How do I tell Dominic, or anyone, what I saw on Wyddial Lane?

I want to be in the living room, in a comfortable chair with my feet up, so that I can think about what to do. This seems an impossible goal. I can't imagine getting to that chair, even though the living room is only a few feet away. Nothing makes sense anymore, so I might as well stay here in the hall, looking at the clumps of mud from Ben's football boots that I'm going to need to pick up at some point.

Where was Georgina Braid? Why wasn't she in the car with her brother and sister? The last thing I saw before I drove away was Flora aiming her remote-control fob at the car to lock it, and then at the gates of her property, which started to glide shut. Maybe Georgina was inside the car and hadn't climbed out yet.

She wouldn't have been able to climb. She's only a few months old. Flora would have lifted her out in her car seat and . . .

I push the thought away, appalled by it. How can I, an intelligent adult woman, be thinking this? Georgina Braid was a few months old *twelve years ago.* She's twelve now. Thomas is seventeen and Emily fifteen. These are facts, not something to speculate about. There is no other possible outcome, for someone who was five in 2007, apart from to be seventeen now, in 2019.

Unless they're dead.

That's not a thought I want in my head either. Thomas, Emily and Georgina Braid are not dead. Why would they be? Two of them can't be, because . . .

Because you've just seen them? Aged five and three, which we've established is impossible? I didn't imagine what I saw. That's impossible too.

Ignoring the mud and the discarded football boots, I walk into the living room and sit down, like someone waiting for something momentous to happen.

There's a clattering of footsteps on the stairs, followed by Zan's voice: "You need to stop blanking Lauren, like, *right now.*"

"Blanking? What does that mean?"

"You'll never understand, Dad, so don't make me explain."

"I'm not blanking her," Ben says. "I'm just not replying to her."

"Yeah, and she's been spamming me all morning about it—so please deal with her, so I don't have to."

The living room door bangs open, hitting the wall. Zannah walks in wearing a black sleeveless top and turquoise pajama bottoms with white spots. There's a lilac-colored towel wrapped around her head and a grainy-textured green substance all over her face. "Mum, can you make him sort Lauren out?" She squints at me. "What's up with you? You look weird."

Great: she's picked today to notice that I'm someone whose behavior might mean something. She stares at me, waiting for a response. In the hall, Dominic is saying that Gary, Ben's football coach, must regret taking Ben off at halftime, because the other team scored their two goals within seconds of Ben being replaced by an inferior defender. This irritates me in a way it wouldn't normally. Dom wasn't there. How does he know? From my brief exchange with Gary at the end of the game, he didn't strike me as a man racked with regret.

"Dad!" Zannah yells. "Come and look at Mum. There's something wrong with her."

The easiest thing would be to say I feel ill. No one would question it. It's hot. I'm not good with heat. It's a joke in our house. Ben and I have pale, Celtic complexions, and constitutions that function better in cooler weather. Dom and Zannah are dark, with olive skin, and love stretching out in the sun for hours at a time.

"Dad, get in here, seriously."

By the time Dom arrives, I've convinced myself that the most sensible thing is to pretend to be fine in the hope that I soon will be. Maybe by dinner time I'll have convinced myself that I didn't see five-year-old Thomas and three-year-old Emily, that the heat made me hallucinate.

"You okay?" Dominic asks me.

"She's *obviously* not okay."

"Zan, can you give me and Dad a minute?"

"What? Why? You're not getting divorced, are you? If you are, can I hit all the people I've been not hitting till now? Callie's parents are splitting up, and she's started punching and pushing me—in a jokey way, but, I mean . . . I have bruises! Actually, I'm so done with that girl."

"We're not splitting up," I tell her.

"Beth, what's wrong?" Dom asks. "Should I be worried?"

From the hall, Ben calls out, "Can you all stop causing drama?"

"Yeah, when we're *dead*," says Zan. "Life *is* drama, little bruth."

"Zannah, please," says Dom. "Upstairs."

"Mum, why can't I stay?"

"Suzannah. We very rarely ask you to—"

"Uh-oh. Dad's full-naming me. It must be serious. All right, I'm going." Zan flounces out of the room, slamming the door behind her.

I still approve of my advice to myself to say nothing and try to pretend it didn't happen, but I know I can't follow it. The words are swelling inside me, preparing to burst out.

"I went to Hemingford Abbots while Ben was playing football."

Dom frowns. "Where's that?"

"Near St. Ives, where football was." I take a deep breath. This isn't the difficult part of the conversation. This bit should be easy. "It's where the Braids moved when they left Cambridge."

"Oh, right. Yeah, I remember—before they moved to Florida."

"What? Who moved to Florida?"

"The Braids did."

The door opens and Zannah reappears. "You're never going to get anywhere at this rate. You need me to interpret." She performs some invented-on-the-spot sign language.

"Were you listening outside the door?" asks Dom.

"Course I was." She rolls her eyes. "Who wouldn't?"

"The Braids didn't move to Florida," I say.

"They did. Something Beach."

"What makes you think that?"

He looks puzzled. "I don't know. I just . . . oh, I know. It might have been LinkedIn. I'm barely on it, but I think I got a message inviting me to follow Lewis, or befriend him, or whatever it is people do on LinkedIn. I had a look at his profile and he was CEO of some company in Florida."

"They might have been in Florida at some point but they aren't anymore," I tell him. "While I was parked outside their house in Hemingford Abbots, a car drove through in the gates. Flora got out."

"I don't know who these people are, but maybe they've split up," says Zannah. "He's in Florida, she's here."

"Zan, please, can you let me talk to Dad alone?" If she hears what happened, she'll either be worried about me or scathingly sarcastic; I want to avoid both.

She looks disappointed, but, for once, doesn't argue. We listen as she stomps back up the two flights of stairs to her bedroom.

"I suppose they might have moved back," says Dominic.

"To the same house? It's the same address they gave us when they left Cambridge twelve years ago: 16 Wyddial Lane."

"They could have rented it out while they went to Florida temporarily. Either way, I'm not sure why it matters. To us, I mean."

"The children haven't aged," I blurt out, aware of how ridiculous it sounds.

"*What?*"

"Thomas and Emily. They should be seventeen and fifteen. Right?"

"Sounds about right, yeah."

"I saw them, Dom. Flora opened the back door of the car and said, 'Thomas! Emily! Out you get!' in a stupid singsong baby voice, and I thought 'Who talks to teenagers like that?' and then the children got out of the car and they weren't teenagers. They were little children."

Dom looks confused. Then he laughs, but tentatively—as if someone might stop him at any moment.

"Beth, that's impossible."

"Yeah. It is, isn't it? I didn't see Georgina . . ."

"Who?"

"Their youngest."

His eyes widen. "Shit—you know, I'd totally forgotten they had a third."

This doesn't surprise me. Lewis and Dom were never as close as Flora and I were. Dom probably hasn't thought about the Braids much since we last saw them.

He smiles. "Remember the two-thousand-pound changing room, in Corfu? That's something I'll never forget."

"I can't believe you didn't tell me they'd moved to Florida."

"Why would I? I deleted the message and forgot about it. We hadn't seen them for years."

"Since Thomas was five and Emily was three." I can't help shivering as I say it, despite the heat. "Which they can't still be."

"No, they can't."

"But, Dom, they *are*. I saw them. I heard Flora call them by their names, I saw their faces. Emily was wearing her 'Petit Mouton' T-shirt. You won't remember it, but . . . Thomas's clothes were the same too. It was them—today, but exactly as they were twelve years ago. And other things were wrong, too."

"Like what?"

I'm grateful that he hasn't laughed in my face, and even more grateful when he sits down next to me and says, "Tell me from the beginning, the whole story."

It's several hours later, and I haven't woken up yet, so I guess it wasn't a dream.

Dom, Zannah and I are sitting at our kitchen table. They're eating Italian food from our favorite local restaurant, Pirelli's.

I'm trying to persuade myself to take a mouthful of the spinach and ricotta cannelloni Dom bought for me. I haven't felt hungry since this morning. Ben is staying overnight at his friend Aaron's house, and is the only member of the family who doesn't yet know what I saw, or what I cannot have seen, depending on your point of view. Zannah knows nearly everything, mainly from sneaking silently downstairs and listening at the living room door.

After wolfing down a shrimp and red pepper pizza, she pushes her plate aside, reaches for her notebook and pen and pulls them toward her. "Okay," she says. "Let's list all the possibilities."

"I had a funny turn because it was hot, and I didn't see what I think I saw."

"When Dad suggested that before, you said, 'I know what I saw.'"

"That's true."

"Mum, you're not making sense."

"If we're listing all the possibilities, we have to include me being . . . wrong. Deluded. However sure I am that I'm not."

"All right." Zannah makes a note. "That's possibility one."

Shouldn't we break it down a little further? A) There was no one there, and I hallucinated three people. B) I saw three people get out of a Range Rover, but they weren't Flora, Thomas and Emily Braid. There's probably a C) and a D) but I can't think what they might be.

"What are the other possibilities?" Zannah looks around the table, like a manager in a meeting waiting for her team to make helpful suggestions. "I can think of one."

"Go on," says Dom. I find it hard to believe we're having this conversation.

"Thomas and Emily, the ones you knew, died. Lewis and Flora then had two more kids, a boy and a girl, and gave them the same names, as a way of honoring the memories of Dead Thomas and Emily."

"Very, very unlikely," says Dom. "Though not impossible, I suppose. It'd explain a lot—the clothes, for example. Lots of families keep clothes their oldest kids have outgrown, and then, if you have more kids . . ." He turns to me. "If the two children you saw today were also Lewis and Flora's, there could well be a strong facial resemblance to Older Thomas and Emily."

"If Thomas and Emily Number 1 are dead, whatever killed them might have killed Georgina as well," Zannah points out.

"There should be an easily found record of it online if they're dead," says Dom.

"No, you're wrong," I say, realizing with a small jolt of shock that I'm supposed to be part of the conversation. This isn't some kind of weird play and I'm not the audience. Dom and Zan are jumping from one thing to another too fast. "*If* Thomas and Emily had died, then yes, Flora might have wanted to have more children, but there's no way she'd give them the same names. No one would."

Dom shakes his head. "There's always somebody who'd do the bizarre thing you think no one would do."

"Not Flora. And . . . I'm not sure anyone would do it. Wouldn't you feel like you were trying to replicate your dead children in a sick way?"

"*I* would, yeah," says Dom. "But I'm not them. Lewis Braid's a weirdo. Always was. Flora wasn't, but . . . if she really did lose her children in some terrible accident, and she's traumatized, who knows what she might do?"

Zannah taps her pad with the pen. "All right, so, option one: Mum had a funny turn and didn't see or hear what she thinks she did. Option two: Mum saw a new, different Thomas and Emily who were named after their dead older siblings. What else?"

I don't feel that option two is in any way a possibility, but I don't have the energy to protest. *Flora wouldn't do that.*

No version of her, past, present, future, however freaked out, would do it.

"Do we want to include a supernatural possibility?" asks Zannah.

"No," Dom and I say together.

"How about: Mum *did* see Thomas and Emily Braid, the same Thomas and Emily Braid she knew twelve years ago, and they're now teenagers, but they look like little kids because they've got some messed-up genetic disease?"

"That's ridiculous," I say.

"There are definitely some conditions that make you age faster, or slower," Zan insists. "If Lewis and Flora both had some kind of recessive gene that was a really bad fit with the other one's recessive gene . . . or something like that. See, Mum? A teacher at school actually taught me something—recessive genes. It might explain who Chimpy is, too."

"How?" asks Dom.

"If Thomas and Emily have both got this genetic thing, chances are Georgina has too. Chimpy might be her nickname. Maybe she needs to live in a home, which would obviously upset Flora, which explains why Mum said she looked and sounded so upset."

"No. This is stupid." Zannah looks hurt, and I feel guilty for cutting her off. I can't stand to think about Flora's children dying or having genetic diseases. I don't want to imagine every possible grotesque scenario. "The two children I saw looked perfectly healthy and normal. There's no—" I break off and start again, trying to sound less dogmatic. "I don't believe there's any medical condition that could make two teenagers look like healthy, normal, much younger versions of themselves."

"Agreed. Overwhelmingly unlikely, verging on impossible," says Dom. "Still, it would explain why they suddenly dumped us as friends. Lewis was obsessed with perfection. He wouldn't have wanted us around to witness the non-growing phase of his children's lives."

"I'm still putting it on the list as option three," says Zannah. "Same Thomas and Emily, genetic condition that makes them look younger. What do Lewis and Flora do? What are their jobs?"

"They're both scientists by training," Dom tells her. "He's been working in IT for years, inventing systems that do all kinds of fancy things. She did the same kind of stuff. They worked together for years, until they had kids, and then Flora gave up her job and became a full-time mum."

"Scientists?" Zannah chews the lid of her pen thoughtfully. "No. Even if a science genius invented a drug that stopped people aging, they wouldn't freeze their kids in time at three and five. Those are pain-in-the-arse ages. You might freeze your kids at, like, nine and eleven."

"Trust me, if Lewis Braid had invented a way to halt the aging process, he'd have patented it, publicized it widely and made millions from it," says Dom. "He wouldn't keep quiet about it."

It ought to be possible for me to listen to this jokey back-and-forth and feel comforted. Instead, it's making me feel lonely. *No one but me saw what I saw.* No one saw how wrong it was. Flora wasn't okay—she didn't look it and she didn't sound it. Nothing about it was right.

"Mum, you've not eaten anything," says Zannah.

"I'm not hungry. You can have it if you want."

"Flora'd be what age now?" Dom asks. "Forty-three, like us?"

"Forty-two," I say. "She could easily have had two more children."

Zannah says, "What about this possibility: Flora *did* have two more kids after her first three. The youngest two look very similar to young Thomas and Emily, because they're siblings, and you saw them and freaked out, Mum. That's why you thought you heard Flora call them Thomas and Emily, but actually she called them by their real names, whatever those are—Hayden, Truelove, whatever."

"No. I heard her say, 'Thomas, Emily, out you get' before I saw their faces."

"Truelove?" Dom raises his eyebrows.

"That's what me and Murad want to call our first baby. Boy or girl."

"Truelove Rasheed?"

"Rasheed-Leeson—I don't know why you'd think I'm ditching my surname, Dad. Think again."

"Truelove? Really?"

"*Did* the Braids dump you as friends?" Zannah asks me. "Why?"

I look at Dom.

"What?" he says.

"I'm waiting to hear your answer."

"I've no idea what happened. All I know is, one minute they were our friends and then we never saw them again."

"Wait, what?" says Zan. "Dad, a minute ago you said they dumped you."

"Well, I assumed . . . Was it us who dumped them?" he asks me.

"By 'us,' do you mean me? You'd remember if you'd been responsible for ending the friendship, presumably." Why am I pushing this? It's the last thing I want to think or talk about.

I need to get away from this for a while.

"Have I done or said something wrong?" Dominic looks at Zannah, then at me. In a different frame of mind, I would find this endearing. Of the four of us, he's always the most willing to accept that something might be his fault.

"Dad has no idea why our friendship with the Braids ended," I tell Zannah, on my way out of the room.

3

I wake up. The curtains in our bedroom are open. It's dark outside, in that thorough way that looks like the night trying to tell you it hasn't finished.

I reach out and pat the top of my bedside cabinet but my phone's not in the place it always spends the night, plugged into the charger. And I'm still in my clothes, lying on the bed, not in it. That's right: I left Dom and Zannah in the kitchen and came in here, when I couldn't stand to hear any more stupid, outlandish theories. I must have closed my eyes . . .

I hardly ever remember my dreams but this time I've dragged a vivid one out of sleep with me: Dominic and I found three new rooms in our house that we'd never noticed before, and were really excited about having more space.

Maybe it was real. Maybe if I looked now, I'd find those three extra rooms. It's no more implausible than what happened in Hemingford Abbots.

Now that I'm less tired, my certainty has returned: I saw them. I saw five-year-old Thomas and three-year-old Emily. Not different children with the same names. I saw the same Thomas and Emily Braid, the ones I knew twelve years ago.

Except that's impossible.

"Dominic?" I call out.

The house responds with silence. I get up, take a sip of stale water from the glass by my bedside that's still half full from God knows when, and go upstairs to where Zannah and Ben's rooms are, and Dom's office. Our bedroom is on the ground floor, with what the estate agent called a "dressing room" attached to it. It's a large, modern room that the previous owners added on. I knew as soon as I saw it that I could add an extra door to make it directly accessible from the hall and it would be the perfect treatment room. Who would want to waste a brilliant space like that on getting dressed?

I told the agent how I planned to use the room. He blinked at me, and continued to refer to it as the dressing room for the rest of the viewing. His final words of wisdom before we left were: "People worry about curb appeal, but bear in mind, the inside of the house is the bit you're going to be seeing day in, day out."

"What a dick." Dom laughed as we drove away. "Does he think we're going to blindfold ourselves every time we get out of the car and walk to the front door? He basically told us he thinks the house is hideous."

I can't understand how anyone could think Crossways Cottage looks anything but beautiful from the outside. Unusual, yes, but lovely. As soon as I saw it, I adored the strange, two-buildings-stuck-together effect. It seemed so perfect for a house on a village green. Half of it's a white-fronted traditional cottage with a thatched roof and the other half is a joined-on barn conversion: black-painted wood. The two completely different roofs meet in the middle, and are different heights—one around a foot lower than the other. The overall effect is charming, not ugly. Unlike all the houses around it, which face the green head-on, ours stands at an angle, hence its name. If we ever have to move, I'll show people around myself instead of leaving it to a useless estate agent. I'll say, "Look how stunning it is—you'll be lucky if I agree to sell you this house at any price."

On the first floor, Zannah and Ben's bedroom doors are wide open. Both of them close their doors whenever they're in their rooms, to remind intrusive parents to stay out. Dom's office door is closed, with a sliver of light visible underneath it. I can hear his fingers tapping at the keyboard.

I push open the door and find him slumped at his computer. "Sit up straight. Your back," I remind him.

"I wondered why it was aching." He stays in the same position, staring at the screen, which is full of different versions of the same logo: three letters twisted artfully around one another, a well-known local company's initials. "Which do you think's the strongest?" Dom asks. "I mean, obviously no one apart from the woman who commissioned them will notice the difference or care, but I have to pretend to have a strong opinion by next week."

"What time is it?"

"Five to . . . uh . . . twelve. Shit. It's nearly midnight."

For the first time since seeing what I saw in Hemingford Abbots, I wonder: could something be wrong with me? I've slept through the whole evening.

No. I'm fine. I needed to recharge, that's all.

Is it? What about seeing the impossible?

"Where's Zan?" I ask.

"She went to Victoria's."

"Is she staying overnight?" It's not unheard of for lifts home to be requested as late as 2 a.m.

"Yup. We can go to bed with no fear of chauffeur duties."

"I've just been asleep for three hours. I'm not tired."

"Well . . ."

"What?"

"I think you're more exhausted than you realize, Beth."

"Dom, I'm wide awake. I've just—"

"I'm not saying come to bed now if you don't want to, but . . . what happened to you today, and then sleeping all evening . . ."

"For God's sake, Dom. You have naps all the time." I'm unreasonably annoyed with him for having the same worry I just had; it makes it harder to dismiss.

"I think you've been stressing out and pushing yourself too hard for too long. You have clients from 8 a.m. till 6 p.m. five days a week. You never take a proper lunch hour—"

"That's a normal working week. We have a huge mortgage to pay off, university costs coming up in a few years . . ."

"I know. I just . . . it's evenings too. You're doing chores and admin till midnight, sometimes."

I wish I could deny it, but I can't. And there's no point saying that he's the one who's working late tonight; we both know that if I hadn't fallen asleep, we'd have spent the evening talking and Dom wouldn't have considered coming up here to work on logos. He'd have gone to bed at half past ten or eleven and . . . yes, I'd then have done a couple of hours of admin. Is there any woman with a full-time job and a family who doesn't need those hours between 11 p.m. and 1 a.m. to catch up and stay afloat? Probably. I don't know any.

Dom has a great talent that I lack: the ability not to give a toss about most things. He regularly announces that some project or other has been delayed, and seems amused by his colleagues' panic over missed deadlines. We've had the conversation dozens of times: me saying that if his work bores him, he should do something else, him telling me I don't understand, and that not caring about his career is his favorite hobby.

He reaches for my hand, squeezes it and says, "I also think you're stressing out about Zannah and Ben more than you realize."

"Zan and Ben are fine."

"I agree. But they're teenagers, and more demanding than they used to be, and you let it get to you in a way that I don't.

Is their school good enough, is Zannah too cheeky and rebellious, is it our fault?"

"No, yes and yes, in that order." I sigh.

"Beth, everything's fine. You know my life's great guiding motto."

"I don't, actually."

"Let it wash over you."

I smile. "You've never told me that before."

"That's because I just made it up."

"But you're right: that *is* your life's guiding motto."

"I wonder if maybe it's not a coincidence," Dom says.

"What?"

"This idea of Thomas and Emily Braid, who are teenagers the same age as ours, being suddenly little kids again." He looks nervous. As if he knows he's taken it too far.

"Wait, are you saying . . ." I laugh. "You think I have a secret desire for Zannah and Ben to be little again, and it made me hallucinate five-year-old Thomas and three-year-old Emily?"

Dom looks suitably embarrassed. "That's crazy, isn't it?"

"Totally. Whatever I saw, whatever happened, it's not that. I think—" I break off, too proud to say it: *I think I'm handling the challenge of parenting two teenagers really well. My kids like me. I like them. How bad can it be?*

"Was Zan . . . okay?" I ask. "When she left, I mean."

"Fine."

"She wasn't worried by . . . any of it?"

"Not at all. I think she's enjoying the mystery. Which I'm a bit closer to solving." Dom smiles proudly, tapping his computer screen.

"You've searched online?"

"Extensively."

So he hasn't been working all evening.

"The good news is, nobody's dead. They're still in Delray Beach, Florida."

"If you're waiting for me to say I didn't see what I saw . . ."

"All I'm saying is, they live in America."

"That doesn't mean they're there right now, today."

Dom frowns. "True," he concedes.

"Maybe they never sold the Hemingford Abbots house. Rich people don't have to sell a house in order to buy a house. They might divide their time between England and Florida."

"You're right. Although . . ." He breaks off with a yawn.

Although, even if the Braids still own the Wyddial Lane house, you didn't see what you think you saw—because that's not possible.

"You should go to bed. Can I . . . ?" I point at his computer. My laptop's in the car. I can't be bothered to go and get it.

"Sure." He stands up. "Look at the search history and you'll find everything I found. It'll make you feel better."

"Only if realizing that I'm having psychotic delusions is a good thing," I mutter, sliding into his chair.

"Well, no one's dead—that's a good thing. And I wouldn't call it a psychotic delusion. More of a—"

"I saw Flora, Dom. And Thomas and Emily, as they were twelve years ago. I saw and heard it all, everything I described."

He squeezes my shoulder. "I'm exhausted, Beth. We'll talk about it again tomorrow. Okay? Want me to bring you up some reheated cannelloni before I go to sleep?"

"No, thanks. I'll get some later." I still don't feel remotely hungry. "Oh—guess what they've called their house."

"Who?"

"The Braids."

"You mean the people living in the house in Hemingford Abbots that used to be the Braids'," Dom corrects me.

"It was named by them for sure, whether they live there now

or not. It's called Newnham House. Typical Lewis. They lived in Newnham in Cambridge, so when they left Cambridge, they called their new house Newnham House, thinking it's a nice way to remember where they used to live."

"And . . . it isn't?"

"No. It's silly. It's clinging to the past in an artificial way—trying to pretend your new place is your old place." When Dom doesn't look convinced, I say, "We also moved out of Newnham. If I'd suggested calling this house Newnham House, would you have agreed?"

I never told Dominic why I wanted to leave Cambridge. Or, rather, I told him, but my explanation was a lie. It had nothing to do with wanting to live closer to my mum, though that's where we've ended up—in Little Holling in the Culver Valley. Mum's about fifteen minutes away by car, in Great Holling. Every time one of her friends pops in while I'm there, she says—and her wording of the line never varies—"What with me living in Great Holling and Beth living in Little Holling, it's like Goldilocks and the three bears!"

I've tried to tell her that it's nothing like that, and that no-body knows what she means. "Of course they do!" Mum insists. Once, Zannah heard this exchange and said to me later, "You're ruder to Gran than I am to you," which made me feel awful.

Mum also doesn't know why I was determined to leave Newnham, having once thought I'd live there all my life. It was because of the Braids. Once they'd left, I couldn't bear the thought of staying there like something they'd discarded, of being the left-behind friends while they moved on to something bigger and better. If they were going to have a new start, then so were we.

"I'd happily swap the name Crossways Cottage for Newnham House," says Dom. "Or for anything less twee. Remember, I suggested getting rid of the name and making do with 10, The Green, but you—"

"Forget it." I wave his words away.

"Beth, I don't see anything wrong about the house name. Sorry. Can I go to bed now?"

He doesn't wait for an answer.

"Night," I call after him.

Once he's gone, I look at his computer's search history: LinkedIn, Instagram, Twitter. He's been busy. No Facebook, though. Why didn't he check to see if the Braids were on Facebook? I haven't either, not once in twelve years. I assumed I knew everything I needed to know about Flora and her family. I knew they'd moved to Wyddial Lane because they sent us a "new address" postcard—nothing personal written on it, just the address, minus the house's name. They must have added that later.

I remember thinking it odd that we'd be on their list; Flora must have known, just as I did, that our friendship was over. Why would she want me to know where she was moving to? Perhaps she thought a complete cutoff would be too stark and obvious; easier to shift to a Christmas-cards-only friendship, allowing us both to pretend nothing was wrong, that we were simply too busy ever to meet.

I go to the bottom of the list of Dom's search results and click on the one he went to first. Might as well follow the same chronological order. I feel more alert than I have for a long time.

It's time to find the Braids.

Lewis is on LinkedIn, though there's no photograph of him, only a gray-man silhouette. So he couldn't be bothered to upload a picture. I skim over the list of his former jobs, several of which he had while I knew him. His current position, "2015 to present," is "CEO of VersaNova Technologies, an application software company based in Delray Beach, Florida."

Dominic was right. How absurd that I needed to see it with my own eyes to believe it, given that my eyes have been seeing the impossible lately, in broad daylight.

Still. Lewis working for a company in America doesn't mean Flora couldn't have been in Hemingford Abbots this morning. *Yesterday morning*, I correct myself. It's after midnight; tomorrow is now technically today.

In Lewis's "Contact Information" there's a VersaNova email address for him, and a link to a Twitter account. Clicking on the link, I find myself staring at his smiling face. The photo that he's chosen to represent him on his Twitter page, the one that appears in a little circle next to each of the short messages he's posted, is of him suntanned and grinning, wearing a black and gray baseball cap.

Like most people, after a gap of more than a decade, he looks older than when I last saw him.

Like everyone except his children, Thomas and Emily, who look exactly the same as they did twelve years ago.

His official name on Twitter is @VersaNovaLewB. I remember Ben joining Twitter and having to choose a name like that. He called himself @boycalledBen, which prompted Zannah to say that she was embarrassed to be related to him.

Lewis's smile is exactly the same: wide and full enough to dimple his cheeks and narrow his eyes, and alarming in its intensity, as if he might be about to start teasing you in a way you're not going to like very much. He used to do that a lot. There was no point in asking him to stop—he'd only do it more. For nearly a year he called Dominic "Rom-com Dom" after we all went to see a movie, *About a Boy*, that Dom liked as much as Flora and I did, despite being a man. Eventually

Lewis professed to find this hilarious, though at first he found it implausible. On the way home from the cinema, he hounded Dom relentlessly: "Really? You liked it? I mean, *liked* liked? You actually thought it was good?"

There's a larger photograph, a kind of personalized banner at the top of his page. This one's a picture of Lewis and two other men in suits and ties, all grinning as if in competition to look the most triumphant. Lewis is in the middle and holding a knife, about to cut into a large, square cake covered in white icing and decorated with blue piped writing. The cake has four candles. Farther down Lewis's Twitter page, I find this same picture again, underneath the words "Happy 4th Birthday, VersaNova Technologies!"

That was posted on January 28 of this year. So Lewis's company is four years old.

"If it looks like it's four, it's probably sixteen," I mutter, then laugh. "Like Thomas and Emily." *Sorry, Lewis. You always hated my sense of humor.*

I'm exaggerating. He didn't hate it, but he didn't understand it either. Any joke that was eccentric or surreal, he used to object to. "But why's that funny?" he would demand. "Tell me. I don't get it." His idea of funny was saying something and then contradicting it a few seconds later, especially if he knew it would disappoint you. The more crushed you looked, the funnier he found it. Like the time the four of us went on holiday together to Mexico. At Heathrow Airport, Lewis grabbed me by the arm and whispered in my ear, "Hey, see that lady over there? She said they were going to upgrade us to first class. Not just business class. *First.*"

"That's amazing," I said. "Do Dom and Flora know?" I couldn't understand why he was telling me alone, when the other two were standing only a short distance away.

"Actually, she didn't say that at all," said Lewis casually.

"I made it up." Then he spent the next hour laughing at my gullibility.

Imagine if he knew that you're gullible enough to believe Thomas and Emily haven't aged in the last twelve years . . .

Dom's words from earlier replay in my mind: "Lewis Braid's a weirdo. Always was."

We liked him, though. Didn't we? We must have. We went on holiday with him more than once. He was one of our best friends.

All the same . . . Now that I come to think of it, I'm not sure I ever wholeheartedly liked him. I was always wary of what he might do or say. I found his confidence impressive, and he had a great line in entertaining rants, but I also felt unsettled by him. He suggested more activities that I felt a strong and defensive need to resist than most people I knew: marathon boozing sessions, terrifying-sounding hikes up the sides of remote mountains, unpleasant prank campaigns against anyone that any of us disliked.

He was interesting and unpredictable, and could liven up a room purely by walking into it.

He had a strange habit of bursting in, like a cowboy crashing into a barroom, about to pull a gun. Instead of a gun, Lewis would typically produce an unexpected declaration of some kind, something that made everyone look up and take notice. It could be anything from "Your lord and king is here, mother-fuckers!" to "Hey, Dom, Beth—your next-door neighbor's wanking over his computer. I've identified the optimal vantage point, if you want to catch some of the action."

He was horrified when we all said we had no desire to watch. "What is wrong with you freaks?" he yelled, actually upset that we were missing out. "It's the most grotesque and embarrassing thing you're likely to see all year! You're a bunch of fucking *philistines.*"

Dom was right: Lewis Braid was weird, and he could be a giant pain in the arse, but we'd have had less fun without him around, no doubt about it. Life would have been much less colorful.

I read a few of the posts he's put on his Twitter page. There's no hint of his more outrageous side here. It's all bland and professional: "Small can be beautiful at VersaNova—great team, fantastic colleagues and a mission worth working for!" "It's a beautiful day for the opening of the ATARM conference here in Tampa, Florida. Proud to be one of the sponsors of this fantastic event, April 18–20!" "VersaNova named in @technovators Top 10 Tech Companies to Watch in 2019" "Great to see our technology director Sheryl Sotork featured in *CapInvest* Magazine" "'Patient Capital Delivers Results'—thrilled to be one of the software companies featured in this article."

I don't know what I was hoping for. *"Hey, guys, it's a bit strange but my oldest two children seem to have stopped growing . . ."*

I keep scrolling farther down, reading tweets from last week, last month, the end of last year. Lewis doesn't post on here very often—only once or twice a month. There's nothing interesting in December last year, or November.

Wait. What's this?

In October, he posted a link to what looks like an Instagram account in his name. I click to open it. I have no idea what a grown man's account might look like. I'm more familiar with Instagram than with Twitter or LinkedIn. Zannah sometimes shows me selfies posted there by girls at her school and asks me if I think they're flames, mingers or donkeys, which apparently, as everyone who is not "so lame" knows, are the only three categories.

Soon I'm staring at a photograph of Lewis on the deck of a boat, with a beautiful sunset behind him. He's been much more

active on Instagram than he has on Twitter. There are a lot of
photos on his page. I work through them methodically, opening
them one by one: Lewis bare-chested in denim shorts, holding
up a fish, Lewis with two other people, walking along a . . .

Two other people.

Are they . . . ?

I try to tell myself that I can't possibly know for certain,
but I do. It's them. It's Thomas and Emily. Teenagers. As they
should be. This is how the children I knew twelve years ago
would look now. When I look at their faces, I have the same
feeling I had when I first saw Lewis's photograph on Twitter:
absolute recognition.

*If this is them, then who were the Thomas and Emily you
saw in Hemingford Abbots?*

Suddenly I feel dizzy, as if I'm tumbling forward without anything to stop me from falling. I hold on to the sides of Dom's
desk with both hands and breathe deliberately until the fuzzy
dots in my head start to clear.

Come on, Beth, get a grip. Nothing has changed, except in
a good way. If these two golden, perfect, healthy-looking teenagers are Thomas and Emily Braid—and they are, I know they
are—then they didn't die and get replaced by a new Thomas
and Emily. And, all right, I still don't know who the two children were that I saw at 16 Wyddial Lane, but I never knew that,
and so nothing has changed, nothing is any more frightening
now than it was before. The Hemingford Abbots children could
never have been Thomas and Emily Braid; they were too young.
I should have known that from the start. I *did* know it, but I
didn't fully believe it—not until I saw these photographs.

Do all Florida teenagers look radiant, sun-kissed and whole-
some or is it just Lewis Braid's children? They certainly all
seem to have a great life in America. Lewis's Instagram is an
apparently endless pictorial log of every pleasure available to

humankind: glasses of champagne, cheese-and-salsa-drizzled nachos, sunsets, beaches, swimming pools, balcony terraces in fancy-looking restaurants . . .

I take in all these things at a glance, but I don't care enough about the details to look at them properly. The Braids are lucky and rich; I knew that already. Now, in Florida, they're luckier and richer. Of course they are.

Thomas and Emily are all I'm interested in. I scroll down, hoping for more photos of them.

Here's Emily in very short black shorts, a long, floaty white blouse and a red-and-navy-blue-bead ankle bracelet. Thomas, in the most recent pictures, has a surfboard under his arm and sun-bleached hair almost down to his shoulders. Unlike his sister, he seems to favor longer shorts, right down to his knees.

His sister . . .

My breath catches in my throat.

Georgina. Where is she?

I search two, three times to make sure. She isn't here. There are no children in these pictures apart from Thomas and Emily. And no Flora either.

Why would Lewis fill his Instagram with many pictures of two of his children, but none of the third? And none of his wife?

A memory surfaces suddenly, from the last time we were all together. Lewis said that if he were Thomas or Emily, he would hate Georgina, because now their parents' sizable estate would have to be divided between three people instead of two. Instantly, Flora looked unhappy. She often used to roll her eyes at him affectionately, as if he were a lovable but disobedient puppy, but this time she looked seriously uncomfortable. He put his arm around her and said, "I'm joking. Relax. There's plenty for everyone."

I only saw Georgina once, but she was a beautiful baby. And Lewis loves to show off all the wonderful things in his life—this

I sigh. "You keep going on about that as if it's some terrible transgression."

"It is! It's crossing a line. You can't do things like that, Beth. It's not good. If you carry on in that vein, anything could happen to you. I don't want to worry every time you leave the house that —"

"Dom. I sat. In. A. car. You're overreacting. Let's not have the same argument we had last night. You win, okay? I'm not going to be making a habit of it. What if I say 'I promise never again to enter a stranger's car or touch their property without permission'?"

"Then I'll be very happy." He exhales slowly. "Right. Good."

I haven't actually said it. I only asked "What if?"

We get out of the car. It's strange to think I'm standing in the exact spot where the three of them stood on Saturday morning: Flora, Thomas and Emily.

Dom presses the doorbell. A few seconds later it opens and a man appears. He's wearing a blue-and-gray-checked shirt tucked into jeans, and white socks, no shoes. He looks at Dominic and me as if we're a delivery that someone has left on his doorstep, which he now has to decide what to do with. He has a square face and mid-brown hair in a short, serious-businessman style.

"Dominic and Beth Leeson?" he says, unsmiling.

"Yes. Thanks so much for agreeing to see us at such short notice," says Dom.

"I agreed for Jeanette's sake. She was disturbed by what happened in the car park yesterday." He looks pointedly at me. "So . . . I'm hoping we can resolve the matter swiftly and avoid any further . . . incidents."

"That's exactly what we want too," Dom assures him. "The last thing Beth wants to do is upset your wife, Mr. Cater. If we can—"

"I think you'd better call me Kevin. And let's not have this conversation on the doorstep."

"Of course not."

"What time is it?" Cater consults a watch that looks expensive. "Yes, it's noon. All right, follow me. Close the door after you."

He takes us through a spotlit lobby that's too sleek and professional-looking to be called an entrance hall. There's nothing homely about it. It's entirely white—like a nonslippery ice rink—and dotted with square pillars. We pass the entrance to an enormous kitchen with a concertina-style door that's standing open. It's made of padded white felt, with rows of silver studs marking out the lines along which it folds. I think it's supposed to look stylish.

There's a hefty white rectangle of kitchen island with a ring of silver pans hanging from the ceiling above it, three beige sofas at the far end of the room, and a wooden table with at least twelve chairs around it, though it's hard to be precise after a quick glance while walking past.

Dom looks back, glares at me and beckons me to hurry up. He thinks I'm snooping and he doesn't want our host to catch me in the act. I wonder if he's noticed: every single thing I've seen so far inside this house could have been chosen by Lewis Braid. Or by the kind of interior designer he'd hire.

Kevin Cater shows us in to a large, rectangular sitting room with unusually high caramel-colored skirting boards, ornate bronze radiators, a herringbone-patterned dark-wood floor, gold floor-length curtains and striped wallpaper: mustard alternating with fawn. Around the room, in a strictly rectangular arrangement, are sofas and chairs, all white, cream or gold, with wooden occasional tables dotted between them here and there.

When I see the framed photographs on the walls, my breath catches in my throat. There are eight in total, and every single one is of a murmuration of many hundreds of birds against a sky. Sunset, broad daylight . . . the skies are all different, as is the shape made by the birds in each picture, but the theme is very much the same.

When I knew him, Lewis Braid used to go wild with glee if he saw a murmuration. I didn't know it was called that until he told me. He would stare and stare, and sometimes chase the birds, and swear loudly, more often than not, when they finally flew out of sight. "Isn't that the most incredible thing you've ever seen?" he'd demand. Once he snapped at Flora for not bringing a camera to a picnic, as if she could have known that there would be a murmuration of starlings above our heads that day. Another time he leaped up and started flapping his arms like an idiot, yelling, "Why can't I be a bird, flying in a beautiful, perfect flock in the moonlight?"

Lewis Braid arranged for these photographs to be framed and hung on the walls of this room. How could it have been anyone else? Does anybody care as much as Lewis does about birds flying in large groups? I've never met anyone else who's even mentioned a murmuration, let alone made a fuss about one.

"Did you do up this room?" I ask Kevin Cater. It comes out harsher than I intended it to.

"Beth . . ." Dom warns.

"It's all right," says Cater. "Actually, we didn't. We inherited it from the previous owners. Everything had been done so beautifully, with no expense spared. Jeanette and I hardly changed anything."

No. Lewis wouldn't leave his murmuration pictures here for another family. He'd take them to Florida. He'd take them with him wherever he went.

Kevin Cater's eyes rest on me a little too long. A smile plays around his lips. It's not a friendly one.

"Take a seat," he says. "I'll go and track down Jeanette. In a house this size, it's easier said than done."

Once he's gone, I walk over to the door and close it.

"Did you see the look he gave me before he left the room?" I ask Dom. "He was taunting me."

"What?"

"He wanted me to get the message: 'If I tell you I haven't changed anything about this house, then you won't be able to prove that the reason it still looks like Lewis Braid's house is because it still *is* Lewis Braid's house.' He's not a good guy, Dom. I don't trust him."

"For Christ's sake, Beth."

"And I don't like him. Did you hear how he said, 'Let's not discuss this on the doorstep,' when *he* was the one who started doing that, not us? And what about 'What time is it? Ah, yes, it's noon, so you can come in'—he virtually accused us of arriving rudely early, when it was easily five past twelve by the time we rang the bell. And he must have known that. If we'd been two minutes early, would he have made us wait outside? That was how it sounded."

"Beth, shut up. I mean it. He's going to walk back in any second now."

"So? I'm not scared of him. Or fooled by him. Everything he's said and done so far is an attempt to manipulate us and make us feel small."

"Shh. Keep your voice down."

"Why? Remember how huge his house is, like he just told us? He's probably in another wing, miles away, and wouldn't hear me if I screamed the place down."

Dom's face is flushed. "I can't be bothered to think of a way to put this tactfully, so I'm just going to say it. You're sounding crazier by the minute. Manipulate us? Come on! The guy's understandably pissed off because he's having to waste his day proving to you that his wife is in fact his wife and not a woman who used to live here and who's currently in Florida. If he's falling a bit short of warm and friendly, that's why."

"Really? If you think that, then you can't possibly understand . . ."

"What?" Dom asks in a whisper. "What don't I understand?"

"You keep saying you agree that everything that's happened is bizarre, but if you really thought that, you'd know that Kevin and Jeanette Cater have to be involved in it, whatever it is. She was wearing the *same clothes*."

The door opens. Kevin Cater walks in, followed by the woman I first met yesterday in the car park in Huntingdon. She's wearing a knee-length black pleated skirt with a red and black leopard-print top and black slip-on pumps.

She's taller than Flora, who's the same height as me. The black trousers she had on yesterday were probably much too short for her legs, but the black boots hid the problem. Convenient for her.

Pleasantries are exchanged by everyone apart from me. The woman offers us drinks; Dom and I both say no. He adds a "Thank you." As I listen to the small talk they're all using to ward off the moment when things might turn awkward, I wonder if Dom has noticed that the Kevin who has returned to the room is considerably friendlier than the one who left it a few minutes ago.

It's all a show.

"So, Beth," says the woman eventually. Is she Jeanette? Didn't Marilyn Oxley tell me that Jeanette Cater had wavy hair, like Flora? This woman's hair is ruler-straight. I wish I could remember exactly what Marilyn said. Not that it matters. Hair can be artificially straightened. "We should talk about what happened yesterday. I . . . perhaps I did not react to you in the best way. I am afraid I was very shocked to find you in my car."

I swallow the urge to tell her it's not her car, it's Flora's. Instead, I say, "I understand. May I ask you a question?"

"Of course."

"Where were you on Saturday morning, and where was your car?"

"I went out, with the children, early, to do some shopping. We arrived back at about nine thirty, I think, or just after."

Her getting the time right means nothing. Marilyn Oxley could have told her what time I returned to Wyddial Lane, or Flora, if she saw me there. I don't think she did, but I can't absolutely rule it out.

"In the silver Range Rover?" I ask.

"Yes."

"Where's your accent from?"

"Beth!" Dom barks at me.

"It's okay," Jeanette says. "The Ukraine. I was born there and grew up there."

"With a name like Jeanette?"

"Actually, that is what I named myself when I moved to England." She smiles at Dominic. "My real name is a full-of-mouth for an English person to say, so . . ." She shrugs.

"I'm so sorry about the interrogation," Dom gushes, determined to ingratiate himself. "I'm assuming you know the, er, situation?"

"Kevin told me what happened, yes." To me, she says, "You were here on Saturday and you saw me with my children. You mistook me for your friend."

"That's right," says Dom. Kevin Cater nods.

I say nothing, determined not to agree with her version of what happened.

"How old are your children?" I ask.

"Five and three years old."

"What are their names?"

"Toby and Emma."

I have the same feeling I had in the car park in Huntingdon: the ground falling away beneath me. Those weren't the names I heard. They weren't the names she called out and it wasn't her who did the calling. Toby and Emma, Thomas and Emily—just similar enough to make me think I could have misheard.

Right, Kevin?

I'll never think that. I don't trust these people. I trust myself: what I saw and heard.

"Which is the older one?" I ask.

"Toby. He is five. Would you like to see a photograph of them?"

"Is that necessary?" Kevin Cater asks.

"No," says Dom, at the same time as I say, "Yes, please."

"It's all right, Kevin." His wife lays a hand on his shoulder as she leaves the room. Kevin takes the opportunity to tell us again how big the house is, which leads to a discussion—one in which I play no part—about whether having too much space can actually be as inconvenient as having too little, if not more so.

Jeanette returns with a photograph in a frame and brings it over to me. I want to scream.

"Well?" says Dom impatiently. "Beth?"

I pass the photograph to him. He holds it close to his face, then at a distance.

"Right, well!" He laughs. He sounds relieved. "These children are *not* Thomas and Emily Braid, I think we can safely say. Not as they are now and not as they were at three and five."

"No, they're not," says Kevin Cater, looking at me. "They're Toby and Emma Cater. *My* children."

Dominic turns to me and says, "I remember quite clearly what the Braid children looked like when I knew them, and these are not their faces."

"I agree," I say. "They're not Thomas and Emily."

"I suppose from a distance, if you were in a car on the other side of the road . . ." Now that he believes I've conceded, Kevin is ready to be generous. "An easy mistake to make, maybe."

"Those aren't the two children I saw. Whoever they are, I've never seen their faces before. Dom, did you notice anything else about that photo—anything interesting?"

"What do you mean?" Dom's face reddens. "Beth, come on."

"What? You think I'm being rude? I asked a simple question: do you notice anything else about the photo?"

"No."

"Like what, exactly?" Kevin Cater snaps.

I stare at him.

"There's nothing to notice, Beth," says Dom. "It's a photo of two children. Come on. I think we've taken up enough of these people's time." He stands up.

Cater follows his lead. Jeanette too. I'm the only one still seated. All three of them are thinking that this will soon be over.

"Who's Chimpy?" I ask Kevin Cater.

"I've no idea," he says. "I don't know what you're talking about." He looks at Jeanette, who shakes her head.

"Means nothing to us," says Kevin. "Sorry."

My sense is that they're telling the truth—but only about not knowing who Chimpy is. About everything else, they're lying. Watching them now, the way they're rearranging themselves, getting into position for the next rehearsed lie, I feel as if we're back in the charade after a small interlude of honesty.

"I hope we were able to help?" says Jeanette.

"Hugely," says Dom.

"I'm not sure your wife agrees." Kevin stares at me.

"Oh, I do," I say, adjusting my tone carefully. "I'm very glad we came. It's been extremely useful."

"I don't want to find you outside my house or in my wife's car again, Mrs. Leeson."

"I know you don't, Kevin. I wouldn't want that either, if I were you."

I'm sitting in my room in the dark when Zannah comes in and switches on the light. "Are you hiding?" she says. "Dad said he couldn't find you."

"He didn't look very hard, then. What time is it?"

"Twenty past ten."

I'm about to say "at night?" but stop myself in time. The curtains are open and it's dark outside. "Ben's not still playing Fortnite, is he?" I ask.

"No, he's in bed—teeth brushed, clean pajamas, room tidied." She smiles proudly. "I am going to make *such* a great parent one day."

"Dad should have sorted Ben out," I say, and it feels like a monumental effort to push out each word.

"Yeah, or you should, as you're his mother," Zannah quips. "Dad's snoring in front of the world's most boring documentary. Mum, what's going on? Dad said you've barely said a word since you left the Caters' house. Are you pissed at him? Was he, like, really annoying?"

I smile. "Not really. He did and said what almost anyone in his situation would do and say."

"So you're all good, you and him?"

"I'm not annoyed with him, if that's what you mean."

"He also said you threatened Kevin Cater."

"Not in so many words."

"But you kind of threatened him."

"Kind of. Nonspecifically. I just let him know that I think he and his wife are creepy liars."

"Mum, you should be careful. At this rate Ben's going to

have to get some of his baddest roadman mates to back you on ends."

"Back me on what?"

"Ugh, you're so old. Never mind. But that's why you shouldn't go around starting trouble."

"Because I'm too old? I'm really not that old, Zannah."

She flops down on the bed next to where I'm sitting. "So what happened then?"

"Didn't Dad tell you?"

"He said the kids living in that house aren't Thomas and Emily Braid, and don't look anything like how Thomas and Emily used to look when they were little."

"We were shown a photo of two young children who looked nothing like Thomas and Emily Braid. That's true."

"So . . . how come you're not saying, 'I made a mistake, it's all over'?"

"Because the more I'm told and the more I see, the more certain I am that I *didn't* make a mistake."

"Fair enough," she says easily.

"Have you been revising?"

She snorts. "No."

"Zan—"

"Tell me about the Greek changing room."

"What?"

"Your Lewis Braid story about the two-thousand-pound changing room in Corfu."

"If I tell you, will you start revising?"

"Definitely. Immediately afterward. All night long." She grins. "Please?"

"It's nothing important or particularly interesting. Just something funny that happened when Dad and I went on holiday with Lewis and Flora to Corfu before you were born. We'd booked an apartment on a beach—literally on the sand, a few meters from the sea, beautiful sandy beach . . . Anyway, one day we went off in search of a restaurant serving better food than what was available nearby. Flora and Dad and I were all fine with the usual tzatziki and olives and stuff, but Lewis was appalled, pretty much from day one, by the quality of the meat at the two tavernas on the beach. He called it 'gray flesh cubes on sticks.'"

"Sticks?"

"Kebab sticks. Anyway, he made a fuss—and when Lewis kicked off, it was impossible to ignore—so we went off looking for somewhere better and we found this hotel. It wasn't exactly posh—really good hotels are in short supply on Greek islands—but it was certainly a step up from where we were staying, and the closest to posh that we were likely to find, and we had a lovely lunch there with meat that Lewis thought was good, but he still wasn't happy. He was always such a perfectionist. Like, *nothing* could be wrong. Nothing unsatisfactory could be allowed to stand."

"He sounds like a twat." Zannah yawns.

"You know what? I think he is, and was, but I somehow didn't fully realize it. I was young and easily impressed and he was so entertaining, and confident. We all just kind of assumed he was brilliant because he acted as if that was beyond doubt. Anyway . . . the hotel's restaurant opened out onto a swimming-pool terrace. Stunning pool: huge, with absolutely no one in it or sitting around it. Apart from us, there were only two other people eating in the restaurant. We got the impression that the hotel was pretty much empty, and by the time we were ready to pay the bill and leave, Lewis was obsessed—completely obsessed, as much as he had been before about finding decent meat—with that swimming pool."

"Why? Shit!" Zannah presses all of her fingers against her forehead, then spreads them out. "I'm trying not to frown, so that I don't get too wrinkly when I'm older. Antiaging moisturizer can only do so much. I've got to train myself to be surprised without scrunching up my face. Why did Lewis suddenly get obsessed with a swimming pool?"

"He said that no holiday was worth going on unless it had a great swimming pool as well as a great beach. He said it as if it was something he'd always thought and passionately advocated, though he'd never mentioned it before. It was so weird. He was the one who'd booked our holiday, chosen the place, everything. He'd happily booked an apartment on a gorgeous beach, with no swimming pool—but only about thirty footsteps from the most stunning, clear blue sea!—and then suddenly he was in the most horrendous mood because going to the hotel had ruined everything for him. Seeing that pool had made him think that his holiday was beyond flawed."

"Mum, he sounds like the biggest arse that ever lived."

"He certainly acted like one that day. He looked as if he might explode with murderous rage at any moment. Dad was taking the piss out of him, Flora was warning him to stop, and I couldn't stop laughing. Then, suddenly, he leaps up from the table and storms over to reception. No one knows what he's planning to do or say. Obviously we follow him, and find him negotiating with the receptionist: why can't we come and swim in their pool every day if we want to, if we eat at the restaurant? No one else is using the pool. The receptionist explained that the pool is for hotel guests only. An argument started, lasting twenty minutes at least, with Lewis insisting that anyone who eats in the restaurant surely qualifies as a temporary hotel guest, and the receptionist saying, no, it doesn't work like that, a guest is someone actually staying in the hotel."

"Ugh. Weren't you horribly embarrassed?" Zan asks.

"Weirdly, no. Anyone watching would have noticed no one but Lewis, so the embarrassment, I figured, was all his. Not that he felt it for a second. Once he saw that his valid guest argument wasn't going to work, he tried another tactic. He asked if we could pay a small fee to come and swim at the hotel, as day guests. The receptionist was nearly in tears by this point."

"I'm not surprised. I'd have said, 'You like our pool so much? I'll be happy to drown you in it, you fucker.'"

"Zan, don't swear."

"Ugh, Mum, relax. What happened next?"

"The receptionist said no to Lewis's day-membership scheme, even after he told her in great detail about various hotels in the UK that allow people to do precisely what he was proposing." I laugh at the memory. "What does a Corfu hotel receptionist care if the Quy Mill Hotel in Stow-cum-Quy, Cambridgeshire, lets anyone buy a day membership for a tenner? She just kept saying, 'My boss not allow, my boss not allow.' It looked as if Lewis was defeated for once—Dad was helpfully pointing that out, saying, 'Come on, Lewis, you've tried your best. Isn't it time to give up now?'"

"Ha! Dad always thinks it's time to give up. Like, even before you've started trying."

"True. But in this case he was right, or at least we all thought he was. Lewis had other plans, however."

"What did he do?"

"Asked if there were rooms available at the hotel. 'You seem pretty *empty*,' he said, stressing the last word."

"As if the receptionist cares," Zannah mutters scornfully. "It's not her hotel. She's not going to get a share of the profits even if it's full."

"I guess. She looked very confused and said, 'You want to stay here?' Lewis said no, he didn't, he had no intention of staying there, but since the only way he was going to be able to use the pool was to book a room, then that was what he'd have to do—that was what the receptionist was forcing him to do. He tried to book two rooms, there and then: one for him and Flora and one for me and Dad. We said not to book one for us, we were quite happy with the beach, but Lewis wouldn't listen. Trouble was, they didn't have two double or twin rooms in the hotel. They *weren't* empty, whatever Lewis thought, and all they could offer us was some kind of self-catering villa in the grounds that slept six people and was part of the hotel but also self-contained. Thankfully, it counted, for pool-using purposes. Dad and I were begging Lewis to see sense and be happy with the beach, not waste his money, but he was a man on a mission. He booked the villa—'the most expensive changing room I've ever used,' he called it later. Two grand, it cost—in 1997. The craziest thing was, none of us slept a single night there, even though it was much plusher than our beach apartment. Again, Dad and I tried our best to make Lewis see sense—since we'd gotten it now, we might as well use it, we said—but he was adamant. He said, 'I want that receptionist to see that she's made me spend two thousand of my hard-earned pounds on a villa that we're going to use for maximum half an hour a day, and for nothing apart from changing into and out of our swim suits.'"

"Okay, I have a theory and a question." Zannah sits up. "You said before, 'Flora was warning him to stop'—in the hotel restaurant. Warning who? Lewis, to stop making a fuss about the pool, or Dad to stop taking the piss out of Lewis?"

"Dad. Flora has always been a peacemaker. A soother-over of potentially troublesome things."

"That's what I thought you meant. Was she scared Lewis would hit Dad or something, if he didn't stop teasing him?"

"I think she might have been, yes. It's hard to explain when you don't know Lewis, but he could get into these weird states, almost like a maniac, and he'd be so full of passionate determination . . . It didn't happen often, but when it did, he could be scary."

"*Did* he ever hit Dad?"

"No. Of course not."

"Why 'of course'? People hit people all the time. How did you get to be friends with a maniac? Unwise life choice."

"Flora was my best friend at university. She was younger than me, but we met through rowing and clicked right away. Lewis was her boyfriend, and I just accepted him, like she accepted Dad. We became a foursome."

"You rowed?" Zannah looks horrified. "In a boat? On a cold, wet river?"

"Yeah, for my college."

"Oxbridge shit is so weird. I'm not going there."

"What, you mean because you're never going to do any revision?"

"Straight savage there from Mum. Nice one, Mum. You really got the crowd roaring with that one."

"Wanna know something I haven't even told Dad yet?"

"Obviously."

"The photograph Jeanette Cater showed me of her so-called children was a fake. It was a picture of a boy and a girl, around five and three. Kevin Cater probably printed it off the Internet. The picture didn't fit the frame. At all. There were big black margins of backing card at the top and bottom. If you'd seen the Caters' house . . . bland, grand, magazine-photo-ready, if you know what I mean—"

"You mean, not a tip like our house?"

"—but perfect, everything fitting exactly right, no expense spared. I don't believe people who live in a house like that would frame a picture of their two children so . . . badly. Yes, our house isn't the tidiest, but even I wouldn't frame a photo in such a slapdash way. Notice, all the photos of you and Ben all over the house are properly framed."

"Why haven't you said this to Dad?"

"I will. I just . . ." I break off with a sigh. "I think he'll tell me that I can't possibly know how two strangers would frame a photograph. And he'd be right."

"Okay, here's my theory." Zan tucks her hair behind her ears. "Lewis—the maniac—used to hit Flora, like maniacs do. She eventually left him, and he let her—maybe he was bored with her and fancied getting a new wife—but he had one condition: she mustn't ever tell anyone that he was a violent abuser. She agreed to keep quiet, in exchange for getting to keep the house. She married Kevin Cater—someone she knew from when they worked together. Lewis moved out of the Hemingford Abbots house and Kevin moved in."

"So Flora Braid is now Mrs. Kevin Cater? Then who's the woman I met, who told me and Dad she was Kevin's wife?"

"The woman with a *foreign accent*?" Zan rolls her eyes. "Don't people with huge mansions usually have foreign servants? Like, Polish nannies, Romanian cleaners? Jeanette sounds more like a French name, to be honest."

"It's not her real name. She said—" I stop, gasp and grab Zannah's arm. "Zan. Zan, you're brilliant."

"Why, thank you. What did I do?"

"I can't believe this has only just occurred to me. Oh, my God."

"What?"

"Do you have a different name for French lessons at school? A French name?"

She laughs. "Er . . . no. Mum, no one calls us anything or teaches us anything at Bankside Park. We don't learn shit." Normally this sort of statement would send me into a spiral of panic.

"My French teacher gave us all French names. I was *Élisabeth*. I told Flora that, soon after we met. It came up when we were comparing notes about the schools we'd gone to, and she said,

'We did that too.' I didn't remember until now. Why didn't I think of it as soon as Marilyn Oxley—"

"Mum, slow down. You're making no sense. So what if you and Flora both had . . . Oh." Zan's eyes widen. "You mean . . . ?"

"Yes. Flora's French name at school was Jeanette."

9

"Great. We're here," says Zannah, as we pull up on the street outside Kimbolton Prep School. "Now are you going to tell me *why* we're here?"

Three nights—mainly sleepless, for me—have passed since I realized that of course Flora would change her name to Jeanette if she were going to change it at all. I've forced myself to do a full two days of massages, so as not to let clients down, and to prove to myself that I'm still an ordinary person with an ordinary life.

It's ten in the morning. I've timed this trip, unlike my last visit to a school, to ensure that I won't bump into any parents dropping off or picking up their children. I don't want to see Flora, or Kevin Cater—or the woman who called herself Jeanette because, for some reason, I'm not allowed to know that Flora still lives in that house.

Today I'm not here to try and catch a glimpse of any of them; I'm here to find out about the people who live at 16 Wyddial Lane—as much as I can, which will be easier if they're not here. I'm telling myself that if I approach the task ahead with the resolve of Lewis Braid on that day at the Corfu hotel . . .

"You can do it, Beth," I hear Lewis's voice in my mind. He was brilliant at motivating people. Once, when I had a deadline at work that was nearly driving me to a nervous breakdown, he said, "Have you tried telling yourself that it's the best fun ever and you're loving every second of it? You'd be amazed by how much that'll change your attitude *and* the outcome."

"But I'm not loving it," I told him. "I hate it. It's nearly impossible."

"So? Can you do nearly impossible things? Yes, of course you can. You *love* to do nearly impossible things." The following day he turned up at our flat with a sign he'd had made for me, saying, in capitals, "WE CAN DO NEARLY IMPOSSIBLE THINGS." "I'm not leaving till it's up on a wall," he said bossily. Would he be a great boss, or the worst in the world? It's hard to know. Both, probably.

"Er, Mother?"

"Sorry, I was just . . ."

"In a trance. I know. So, why are you so sure the Braid-slash-Cater kids go to this school?"

Excellent question. When I have to explain to Dom later why I let Zannah come with me when I should have made her stay at home and spend her pre-GCSE study leave revising, this is what I'll tell him: she's got a sharp mind and a powerful capacity to get to the heart of a problem. Nothing associated with school ever brings this out in her. Thinking about the Braid-slash-Cater problem does.

"I know what type of school Lewis would pick for his kids," I tell her. "This type—of which this is the closest example to Wyddial Lane."

"But they might not be Lewis's kids."

"I trust what I saw," I repeat my mantra. "I saw Thomas and Emily Braid, aged five and three. Or, at least . . . two children who looked so similar to them that they can only be Lewis and Flora's."

"What school did the other, older Thomas and Emily go to?"

"Thomas had just started at King's College School in Cambridge when we last saw them. Emily was signed up to go there too."

"Mum! Then that's where we should be."

"I thought about it."

"And?"

"Why would Flora have been in Huntingdon doing chores on a school-day morning? She wouldn't. If Thomas—new Thomas—is at King's, she'd drop him off, then do those chores in Cambridge. Bank, post office, nipping to a shop . . . whatever. Why would she drive to Huntingdon?"

"Major logic fail," says Zan. "She could have gone to Huntingdon for a million reasons. Maybe she's got a friend who works there and they were meeting for lunch, or—"

"No. She was coming back to her car in the car park long before lunchtime."

"Coffee, then."

"It's possible, but . . . I don't know. I just figure: someone who's in Huntingdon on a weekday morning is more likely to have a child here, at this school, than at a school in Cambridge. All other things being equal."

"Yeah, but all other things about this situation are so *not* equal, are they? All other things are, like, totally fucked."

"Zannah, stop swearing." I turn to face her. "I mean it. You need to behave properly. Not only to please me and Dad, but because you want to go out into the world as—"

"Mum, stop trying to cram years of proper parenting into one little pep talk. You're not a Mumsnet kind of mum, so don't pretend you are."

I don't know what she means because I've never looked at Mumsnet. Actually, maybe that's what she means.

"Do you want to come in with me?" I nod in the direction of the school.

"Sure—but to do what? No school's going to answer questions about its pupils from someone who just walked in off the street."

"Which is why we can't ask questions. We have to pretend to know already. What's tricky is working out *what* we're going to pretend to know."

"What do you mean?"

"Come on, let's go. I've got an idea. Your job is to stand behind me and smile, looking like the respectable daughter of a respectable mum. And no swearing. First we need to grab something from the boot that might belong to a five-year-old boy." My car's boot operates as a kind of storage cupboard-cum-dustbin. There's plenty in it to choose from.

Five minutes later, armed with a pale blue drawstring sports bag with a pair of socks inside it, Zannah and I are standing at the reception desk of Kimbolton Prep School. I press the buzzer and wait, rehearsing what I'm about to say.

A woman appears. She's young and elegant, with short hair, a long slender neck and lovely earrings: small round pearls that look real, with solid silver flower shapes behind them. She reminds me of a swan, and looks friendly enough. "Can I help you?" she says.

"Yes, I hope so," I say with a smile. "I'm a friend of Jeanette Cater's. She left this in my car boot . . ."—I wave the bag in the air—"and I don't have time to go to her house now and drop it off, so I thought . . . would it be okay to leave it with you?"

"Sure. No problem at all."

I fight the urge to say, "So you know Jeanette Cater, then? Her son is here, at this school?"

The receptionist reaches for a pad and pen that are over on the other side of the desk. "Let me write down your details, just so I can tell Jeanette what happened."

Shit.

"Beth Leeson," says Zannah cheerfully, while I'm frantically

trying to think of a fake name I can give. *Too late now.* "Oh—
sorry, that's my mum. She's Beth Leeson. I'm Zannah."

I try to look unflustered. Zan's probably right: better not to
lie. Besides, if the receptionist hands Jeanette Cater a random
sports bag later and tells her it was brought in by a person
whose name she doesn't recognize and who claims to be her
friend, it's going to be pretty obvious who's behind it—especially
when Jeanette asks for a physical description of this mysterious
woman. My hair is half brown and half blond at the moment;
for months I've been too busy with clients and their problems—
both physical and emotional—to get it sorted out.

Zan must have worked this out long before I did: I've been
lied to, and I'm taking steps to find out why, and what's really
going on. I'm not ashamed of any of my actions and, by doing
this, I'm letting Jeanette Cater know that I'm not.

It's funny how quickly my thinking patterns have adjusted
to all the unknowns. When I think about "Jeanette," there's a
shadowy person in my mind who might be either Flora or the
woman with the foreign accent. When I think about "Thomas
and Emily," sometimes they're the two photogenic teenagers on
Lewis's Instagram and other times they're the two small children
I saw getting out of the silver Range Rover last Saturday.

The receptionist writes down "Beth Leeson." "Phone number?" she asks me.

"Jeanette has my number."

"Oh—ha, yes. Sorry! I'm so used to taking full details from
people. Tell you what, though . . . if you could just let *me* have
your number, just in case?"

Zannah recites our home number, and the receptionist writes
it on the pad. When she looks up, I see uncertainty in her eyes.
"And you're Jeanette's . . . *friend*?" she says, as if this is an
outlandish concept.

"Yes."

Two spots of red have appeared on her otherwise white cheeks. She holds out her hand awkwardly to take the sports bag from me. She's gone from friendly and confident to nervous in the space of seconds. Why? "What's your name?" I ask her.

"Lou Munday," she says quickly. "Rhymes with the famous song, 'Blue Monday'! Haha. My husband says that's one of the reasons he married me." She's still on edge, but trying to hide it.

I pass her the bag.

We say our good-byes, and Zannah and I are halfway to the door when she calls after us, "Thanks again! I'll give this to Jeanette later when she comes to collect Thomas."

I freeze. Zannah and I exchange a look.

Thomas. Not Toby.

Kevin Cater lied. I now have proof, and it came from someone impartial, with no skin in the game. I should make a motivational sign like the one Lewis made for me, with "I trust myself" emblazoned across it, and stick it on the wall in my treatment room. My clients would love it. Lots of them are keen on positive psychology and mindfulness and things like that.

Zan is ahead of me, walking back to reception. "Did you say Toby, Mrs. Munday?" she asks in her fake-sweet voice, the one she only uses on me when she wants me to spend serious money on her. "Jeanette's son isn't called Toby. He's called Thomas."

"I know. I said Thomas." She looks confused.

"And his sister's not called Emma," I say.

"No, she's called Emily. I didn't say anything about an Emma." The red spots on her cheeks are growing.

"I know you didn't. Can I tell you something that's going to sound—"

"Mum," says Zan curtly. She's trying to warn me off.

"No, I'm doing this," I say. "Mrs. Munday—"

"Please, call me Lou."

"I don't know how well you know the Cater family . . . for example, do you know that Thomas and Emily have a younger sister called Georgina? A baby?"

"We don't know that's true," says Zannah.

Lou Munday looks mystified. She says, "The Caters don't have a baby called Georgina, or any baby at all. They just have Thomas and Emily."

"Just to check: we're talking about Kevin and Jeanette Cater, who live at 16 Wyddial Lane, Hemingford Abbots?"

Lou has started to pluck at the skin of her neck with the fingers of her right hand. "I probably shouldn't . . . I mean, I *can't*. I can't tell you where they live."

"I've just told you where they live: 16 Wyddial Lane, Hemingford Abbots. Is that right?"

She starts to mumble about safeguarding issues. It's been a while since she looked me in the eye.

"Does Jeanette Cater have a foreign accent?" Zannah asks her.

"A foreign . . . No, she . . . I'm sorry, but I'm afraid I can't—"

"No? No foreign accent?"

"Zan, wait. Lou, I'm really sorry about this. I don't want to make you feel uncomfortable, and obviously you don't have to tell us anything else. We'll leave in a minute, I promise. Before we go, though, I'd like to tell you something. Tell, not ask."

Am I really going to do this? Is this a strategy, or a burst of recklessness I'll regret?

"I lied to you. I am Beth Leeson—that's true—but the bag I gave you belongs to my son. It's nothing to do with the Caters. I lied because . . . well, it's a long story, but . . . I think there might be something wrong—I mean really, horribly wrong—in the Cater household. It would take too long to tell you everything so I'll just say this: three days ago, Jeanette Cater, or, rather, a woman who introduced herself to me as Jeanette Cater, with a foreign accent, told me that her children were called Toby and Emma. Not Thomas and Emily. And . . . a few days before that, I saw a woman *who is not Jeanette Cater*, because she's my old friend Flora Braid, getting out of a silver Range Rover and . . ." I should probably stop there. The rest would sound too implausible.

Lou shakes her head. "I can't talk to you," she says in a tight voice. "You need to leave."

"You have my phone number. Will you ring me later? I swear to you, whatever you tell me will go no further. No one will ever know you said anything at all."

She shakes her head more vigorously. The pearl flowers on her earlobes jiggle up and down.

"I'm worried about the children. Thomas and Emily. I think you are too."

That one hit home. Her eyes widen. She takes a step back and nearly trips over the sports bag, which she's left on the floor. She picks it up and pushes it across the desk to me. "Please just go," she says.

10

The plan was to drive straight home after Kimbolton Prep School; the decision to ignore the plan was unanimous, which is why, for the third time in less than a week, I'm on Wyddial Lane. I turn the corner and pull over as soon as I'm clear, at the top end of the road. Hopefully Marilyn Oxley won't see me, or the Caters.

Or Flora.

Zannah says, "If I pass my test when I'm seventeen, will you and Dad buy me a car? I want a Mini."

"Too expensive," I say. "But I'll buy you driving lessons—which otherwise you won't be able to afford—"

"Cool."

"—if, and only if, you start revising properly for your GCSEs. Tomorrow, first thing."

"Blackmailer."

I feel as if the ever-vigilant eyes of Marilyn Oxley are on me already. If they're not now, they soon might be, even if I stay up at this end of the street. She's probably got a long-range camera fitted to her roof and a bank of screens in her front room—like security guards in films, who always fall asleep at the exact moment that a balaclava-clad psychopath tiptoes through all the rooms they're supposed to be watching. Those movies need Marilyn Oxley; she wouldn't miss a thing.

I don't care if she sees me. I'm here to talk to other people, not her, and certainly not Kevin Cater and Fake Jeanette. I'm allowed to do that—or allowed to try, anyway. Today, my target is all the other houses. I need to find residents of Wyddial Lane that I haven't already spoken to.

"Can I come with you?" Zannah asks. "Or will that make us look like Jehovah's Witnesses? They always go in pairs."

"I don't think there's much chance of anyone thinking you're doing the Lord's work," I say, eying her gray T-shirt, which has "Gang Sh*t" printed on it in black. How did I not notice that before? "If you're coming with, you'll need to zip up your jacket," I tell her. "Did you have it zipped while we were talking to Lou Munday?"

"Irrelevant, since that's in the past." Zan snorts dismissively. "What, you think she'd have spilled everything she knows if I'd worn a Bambi T-shirt instead? Anyway, there's an asterisk, so it's not even a swear word. Which house shall we start with?"

"Let's just go door to door."

"Let's definitely *not* do that. We should pick the ones that look most chilled."

"Chilled? Oh, you mean—"

"Not refrigerated. Most of them look uptight and closed off—walls, fences, high gates. Kind of like luxurious prisons. There's no way people who live in houses like that are going to invite two strangers in and start chatting to them, answering a load of weird questions."

"So shall we start with the only one up at this end that doesn't look like that?" I point at it through the car window. On one of its gateless gateposts, there's a sign saying "No. 3." There's a wall, but it's low and crumbling. There's nothing to suggest that its owners want to hide themselves from prying eyes.

"Number 3 looks a good shout," Zan agrees. "Especially as it's got a wheelie bin at an angle outside its front door."

"Why? How's that relevant?"

"Think about it, Mother."

We sit in silence for a few seconds. Then I say, "Thought. Still don't know."

"It can't be bin day, or everyone's bins would be out on the pavement. Or a good few still would, at least—the ones belonging to people who aren't yet back from work. All these houses have massive gardens, loads of space on either side. But number 3's owners couldn't be bothered to wheel the bin a few feet farther and put it there, in that wooden bus-shelter type thing attached to the side of the house that's probably a bin store. They'd rather make the least possible effort, and leave it at the top of the driveway, where it makes the house look worse to anyone who passes by. I mean, who cares, right? I wouldn't either. There are bins in the world—deal with it."

"But that's your point," I say, getting it at last.

"Uh-huh. Number 3's owners can't be bothered with trivial shit. All their neighbors hate them for lowering the tone with their noticeable bin, and they don't care. Maybe they also won't care that it's not the done thing to tell strangers about what secret, twisted things your neighbors get up to."

"Okay. Number 3 it is."

I lock the car and we walk up the driveway. It's a wide house, as enormous as all the others on Wyddial Lane, painted the color of buttermilk, with a redbrick chimney attached to its front. Next to the front door there's a sign that says "Low Brooms."

I ring the bell and we wait. "We might have to wait a while," I mutter. "Getting to the front door in a house this size . . ."

It opens surprisingly quickly. A woman who looks around my age, wearing cut-off bleached-denim shorts and a pink long-sleeved top, smiles at me and Zan and says, "Please say something nice!"

Not the response I was expecting.

Her frizzy brown hair has streaks of gray in it. Around her neck, on a leather cord, she's wearing a huge silver pendant that looks like a jellyfish, with a shiny dark green stone at its center. "I like your pendant," I tell her, hoping that's nice enough.

She beams at me. "That's the *best* thing you could have said. You can come again!" She laughs. "I couldn't adore it more, and I've worn it every day since I bought it and, do you know what? *No one* has said anything about it apart from you. No one's spontaneously said, 'What a beautiful piece of jewelry!' Look, it's two-sided. Nautilus with a malachite eye on one side, ammonite fossil on the other. Oh—that wasn't what I meant when I said, 'Say something nice!' I wasn't fishing for compliments!"

"Jellyfishing for compliments," I say, trying to present myself as the sort of person this woman would get on well with.

"Huh? Oh! No, a nautilus is very different from a jellyfish. Though in the grand scheme of things, they're both in the sea, so . . . hey!" She shrugs. "I'm sorry. You must think I'm high on drugs. I'm really not. I'm just kind of excited. I don't normally . . . wow, I mean, *shut up*, Tilly, stop blathering on at these poor people!"

"Hi, Tilly. I'm Beth Leeson. This is my daughter, Zannah." I hold out my hand. She shakes it. "Please don't stop blathering on our account. We came here to blather, as a matter of fact, so . . . if you blather first, I'll feel less guilty about my own blathering!"

I can feel disapproval radiating from Zannah. As soon as we're alone, she's going to list all the ways I handled this wrong.

Tilly from number 3 appreciates my act, anyway. She's laughing like a loon. "Okay, well, do you wanna come in?" she says. "Assuming you're not serial killers, or canvassers from an evil political party? They're all evil these days, let's face it. I'd vote Lib Dem but there are only about three of them left and one's a golden retriever." She throws back her head and cackles again.

"We're neither murderous nor political," I tell her.

"Fantastic. Come in, then." We can't. She's blocking the

doorway. "I'll tell you what I meant. So. For months, I've not been answering the door when the bell rings. Justin and the kids are out all day during the week, and I've got those hours and *only those hours* to do all my work—I work at home—and clean, and cook, and the rest, you know how it is. So, my New Year's resolution was: no more rushing to the door when the bell rings. I stuck to it, too. Religiously. Unlike my other resolution, which was to cut out sugar and flour and alcohol, but hey! And at first it was *so liberating*. Understanding for the first time in my life that my doorbell—like my phone, like my email inbox—is there *to serve me*. Not the other way around! You know? And it's been amazing, I've been so productive since January, but . . . lately, I've started to think it's a shame. Who knows what those doorbell rings might be, you know? What if I'm too willingly closing myself off to new, fantastic experiences? So today, on an impulse, I thought to myself—I needed a break, to be honest—'Get off your bum and open that door.' And immediately panicked in case it was something dull like a survey about shopping habits. I never shop, anyway. Hate it. Waste of a day."

"If you want the opposite of dull, you're in luck," I tell her. "I rang your bell in the hope that you'd answer a whole load of . . . unusual questions that no one else will answer honestly—about Wyddial Lane."

"What kind of unusual?"

"It's a long story. The short version is, I had some friends who used to live at number 16, and—"

"Number 16. That's the Caters, right? And before that . . ." She stops. Her eyes widen. "Lewis Braid? Is he your friend?"

"Not anymore, no. Not for twelve years."

"But you're here to ask unusual questions about him? Please say you are! That man is *crying out* to have unusual questions asked about him. Well, the opposite actually—he's not crying out for it, he'd hate it, but the world is, or at least, I am."

"I am too," I say.

She moves to one side and waves us in. "I'm so glad I opened the door," she says as we follow her across a wide entrance hall and into a messy kitchen with a red Aga and many blobby children's paintings stuck up on the walls. "This was meant to be—I truly believe that. Time to rethink that resolution!"

I try not to stare at the most eye-catching thing in the room: an enormous and scary-looking wall-chart calendar with boxes for all the days of the year, and black-and-white drawings of branches and leaves wrapped around them. There's tiny, spidery handwriting in many of the boxes in four different colors: red, green, purple and orange. It's weirdly beautiful, as long as you don't need to read the writing.

On a battered pine table at the center of the room, papers and forms are spread out. They look confusing and boring. Tilly's work, presumably. She sweeps them to one side, saying, "Fuck off, boring company tax returns!"

Does that mean she's an accountant?

"Okay, let's get this kettle on," she says. "Tea? Coffee? Rubis? And feel free to fire questions at me while I make drinks."

"What's Rubis?" I ask.

"You've not discovered Rubis? Oh, my good God! I'm about to become your favorite person. Oh." She frowns. "You're driving, probably. It's alcoholic."

"Tea for me, thanks," I say.

"Rubis is *heaven*. Imagine the most yummy chocolate that's *also* a delicious velvety red wine."

"I'll have some," Zannah says sweetly.

"You do right—as we Yorkshire folk like to say!" Tilly beams at her.

"Just a tiny bit," says Zannah's killjoy mother. Yorkshire? Tilly's accent couldn't be less northern if it tried.

She hands Zannah a bottle and glass, then puts the kettle on. I tell her a much-curtailed version of the story so far: that I saw Flora at number 16 and in Huntingdon, and that, despite this, the Caters and Lewis have all insisted that Flora's in America.

"Huh. Interesting," says Tilly. "As far as I know, they live in America now. Is it possible Flora was back, or is back, to visit the Caters?"

"Yes, but then why would everyone lie? On the phone, Lewis didn't say, 'Yeah, you might well have seen Flora, she's in England at the moment.' Flora herself rang me and said she was in Florida—no mention of any trip to Hemingford Abbots. And when I told her I was sure I'd seen her outside her old house, she said, no, no way, impossible. She ended the phone call after about ten seconds, having promised to ring me back, which she didn't. And then the next day, I bump into her in a car park in Huntingdon."

"That is deeply, deeply peculiar," Tilly says, handing me my tea. "Lewis is, though. Or was when I knew him. Maybe his wife is too. Maybe she was back, and didn't want to see you. Nothing against you, just a case of 'This particular trip is about *this* and I don't want to use any of it to do *that*.'"

"That'd explain her saying, 'How's things? Hope all's well! Gotta dash.' But lying about what country she's in when she knows I've seen her? And Lewis lying, and the Caters lying?"

"You're right," says Tilly. "No one would go to those lengths to avoid maybe having to have a coffee for half an hour with an old friend they'd rather not see."

Zannah says to Tilly, "You said before that maybe Lewis's wife is weird too, because Lewis is weird. Didn't you know Flora, when they lived here?"

"No. That was one of the weirdest things about Lewis: his

wife, whom he worshipped—but no one ever saw her! It was the talk of the WLRC."

"What's that?" I ask.

"Sorry. Wyddial Lane Residents' Committee. We all decided Lewis's wife was a hermit who never left the house. Lewis was very sociable—came to every meeting and every drinks do, sometimes with his kids—but never invited anyone over to his place. *Ever*. Normally, that would make you unpopular—very keen on proper turn taking, is the WLRC; drives me crazy! Sometimes I can't face hosting a party for forty people! So shoot me!—but everyone loved Lewis because he'd make every party a success. He was a one-man show—and a brilliant one, too. And he'd always arrive laden down with booze and cakes and treats. But . . . yeah. We all wondered about the invisible wife. He talked about her nonstop but it was almost as if . . ."

"As if he wanted to make her feel like a presence in spite of her absence?" I suggest.

Tilly slaps me on the arm with the back of her hand. "That's it *precisely*. That very thing."

"Even if she didn't come to events, people must have seen her, though."

"Yeah. One or two did report having seen a dark-haired woman driving out through the gates but that was about the extent of it. And, actually, it's maybe unfair to label Lewis an oddball since *she* might well have been the weird recluse, and he was covering for her, trying to present a show of normal family life, but even if that was the case, what he did later . . ."

"What did he do?" Zannah asks. I notice that her glass is full. Last time I glanced at it, it was empty. I pick up the Rubis bottle and move it away from her.

"If I tell you, you must never tell anyone. Swear on all you hold dear. I've never told anyone on Wyddial Lane. Only Justin, my husband."

Zan and I promise not to tell anybody.

Tilly leans in conspiratorially. "He *stalked* me. Obsessed with me, he was. Lewis Braid, perfect husband and dad, turned into an honest-to-God creepy stalker."

"What? *What?*" says Dom, when I come to the bit about Lewis stalking Tilly. "I simply don't believe that. Sorry. No way!" His protests are so loud that I have to hold my phone away from my ear. Zannah and I are in the car in a service station car park on the A14. I'd been fobbing Dom off all day with quick, jolly "All fine! Talk later!" replies. I would have waited until we got home to tell him all this, except I've changed the plan again. Driving home isn't next on my agenda anymore.

"Why don't you believe it?" I ask him.

"I mean . . ." I hear something crunch in the background at his end, and picture him at the kitchen table, eating an apple. "I just don't."

"I want to hear why. It'll confirm what Zan and I think. Spit it out. Don't worry about being ungallant."

"You said she had frizzy hair, brown streaked with gray?"

"The essence of frizzy! So frizzy, you could barely see the individual strands of hair. If she's ever used conditioner, I'd be surprised."

"Did she have a pretty face?"

"She had a pleasant face, I'd say."

"Thin? Fat?"

"Neither. Maybe about like Mrs. Adlard."

"Who's that?"

"Dominic," I say flatly.

"What?"

"Mrs. Adlard is Ben's tutor."

"Oh, her. Right. So, not thin."

"But not fat either. Like, maybe a size 14."

"Lewis would think that was fat," Dom says without missing a beat. I give Zan a thumbs-up sign. One more subscriber to our opinion; we must be right. "If Lewis was going to stalk a woman, he'd pick a skinny, beautiful one. Someone who looked like Flora used to look before she had three kids."

"Zan and I agree. And he might pick that skinny, beautiful woman to stalk *because* Flora no longer looked exactly the way she did before she had three kids—he could easily be that shallow, with his constant search for perfection—but what he definitely would never do is become obsessed with a plain-but-pleasant-looking, not-thin, frizzy-haired, *gray*-haired person."

"Never."

"But I'm sure Tilly was telling the truth, that's the problem."

"She was," Zannah confirms. "Mum, put it on speaker. Aaand you have no idea what that means. Pass it here."

She fiddles with my phone, then balances it on the armrest between us. "Speak, Dad," she orders.

"Hello! Testing, testing."

"So lame. See, Mum, now we can both hear him. Dad, she said they'd always been friendly, and Lewis helped her set up her own business, went above and beyond, came around at all hours of the day and night to provide support—but she didn't think anything of it because he was helpful to everyone, he was just that kind of guy."

"He was," says Dom. "That's true. He couldn't stand for anything to fail, and that included his friends' projects. Remember when I ran the marathon, Beth?"

"What happened?" asks Zan.

"Lewis nearly fell out with me because I wouldn't let him be my coach and personal trainer—even though he had a full-time job, wasn't a sports coach and had never run a marathon himself. Still, he wanted to take time off from work to make sure I succeeded and would barely take no for an answer. He couldn't imagine me being able to do it without his help. I did, though, and he was genuinely happy for me."

"At the same time as going on for months about how you'd have finished much faster if you'd let him coach you," I say.

"Sounds like how he was with Tilly's business," says Zan. "She thought, great, what a nice friend. Her business did well. The Braids moved. But he still kept turning up outside her house, *after* he'd moved to Florida—spying on her from his car. The first couple of times it happened, he made crap excuses—like, really crap. One time she found him in her back garden and he said he'd been passing and heard something that sounded suspicious, so he'd gone to investigate. Another time she found him asleep on a bench in her back garden. On his chest was guess what? A pair of Tilly's silk pajama bottoms that she'd left to dry on the washing line."

"And . . . all this happened after the Braids moved to Florida? When the Caters owned the house?"

"Yeah, and when Lewis was working in America," I say. "Tilly, thinking it was all very odd, googled him and found that he definitely had a job in Florida at the time . . . but he also kept making time to come back and . . . fall asleep in her garden clutching items of her clothing."

"It all came to a head after the silk pajamas," Zannah tells Dom. "Tilly and her husband confronted him, told him they weren't going to pretend to believe any more excuses, and he broke down in tears and admitted it. He *cried*, Tilly said. Wept buckets."

"What did he admit?" asks Dom.

"That he'd fallen in love with her!" Zannah slurs. "He actually said that to her and her husband. Begged them never to tell anyone, especially not his wife, and swore blind that he'd never do it again. Which he didn't. The silk-pajama time was the last stalking episode."

"Zannah, you sound drunk. Beth, what's wrong with her?"

"Tilly gave her some booze."

"For Christ's sake, Beth!"

"Yeah, Mum." Zannah grins at me. "This happened on your watch. You tell her, Dad."

"Can you two come home now, please?"

"Not immediately. Dom . . . is it possible that there are two sides to Lewis? What if the perfection-seeking side of him makes him miserable, with the pressure it piles on? Tilly's dynamic, happy, relaxed. Doesn't give a damn about a few gray hairs."

"And Lewis had a secret urge to abandon his perfect life and run off with her? I mean . . . I'm not saying it's not possible, because anything's possible, but . . . Why aren't you coming home? What else are you doing?"

"Going to Wokingham. I need to try and find Flora's parents. They must know something about what's going on. Lewis Braid has been their son-in-law for twenty years."

"Her parents? Beth, you don't *need* to do that."

"I want to."

"Please don't. Beth, the time comes when you have to draw a line. That time has come. Now. Today. Zannah needs to get back here and start revising. She's on exam study leave, not . . . crazy-dashing-around-the-country leave. Ben wants you to come home."

"Straight after Wokingham, I promise. Zannah was desperate to come with me, Dom. She's really interested in this."

"That's what worries me."

"No revision would have happened even if I hadn't brought her with me. You know as well as I do—she'd have done fuck all apart from paint her nails and watch reruns of *Love Island*."

"Hashtag when your parents believe in you," says Zan with a chuckle.

"She's got a brilliant mind and today, all day, that mind has been *working*." I was planning to say that anyway, but now it looks as if I only said it to ingratiate myself. Zannah makes a face at me.

"Do you want to hear what happened at Kimbolton Prep School?" I ask Dom.

Without waiting for his answer, I launch into a full account. He may be right: there might be a point at which one ought to draw a line, but I'm hoping there's also a point at which any intelligent person realizes that they have to find out what the hell's going on or it'll bother them forever. I reached that point some time ago.

I describe my conversation with Lou Munday.

"That all sounds . . . strange, horrible and worrying," Dom says when I've finished.

"Yep. I'd swear that secretary wanted to tell me *something*— more than she told me. Zannah agrees."

"I'm not sure I do," she says unhelpfully. "Maybe. Maybe Lewis Braid stalked her too."

"She didn't give me the brush-off in a normal, routine, off-you-go-you-nut kind of way. There was something she could have told me if she'd wanted to, if she'd not been scared of losing her job."

"Or scared of getting involved in something really unpleasant," says Dom. "Which you should be too, Beth. Whatever's going on in that house and with the Braids and the Caters, it's something our family needs to keep out of. Think about everything you've told me so far—Tilly, now the school stuff— it all adds up to a giant neon sign saying 'Stay the hell out of this mess.'"

"Typical graphic designer response there from Dad," says

Zan. "Bringing signage and the visual into everything. Me and Mum aren't graphic designers so we can't see that sign."

Dom makes a disgusted noise. "Kevin and Jeanette Cater told us their children were called Toby and Emma."

"Uh-huh. And, don't forget, she turned up at the car park wearing the same clothes Flora was wearing less than an hour before. Oh—and she isn't Jeanette Cater. Lou Munday told us Jeanette doesn't have a foreign accent. I forgot that bit."

"Who's that?"

"Memory of a goldfish," Zan mouths at me.

"Oh, the school secretary. Right. Well, whoever the woman at Newnham House was, she and Kevin Cater, assuming that's his real name—"

"Yeah, they fed us a load of bullshit," I say. *And you thanked them for it.*

"To our faces? While smiling and supposedly trying to help sort things out? I guess they must have, but . . . that's pretty twisted, isn't it?"

After more than forty years on this planet, Dominic has trouble believing that a civilized and solvent couple with an immaculate house could lie to him. He's still keen to believe in a version of the world in which everyone has each other's best interests at heart.

"They flat out lied." He still can't believe it.

"Yes. Dom, I have to go. I'll see you later tonight, okay? Bye." I press the end-call button before he can give me any more reasons for why I should come home right away.

11

Three hours later, we're parked on Carisbrooke Road in Wokingham, outside a house that I hope still belongs to Flora's parents. I only came here once with Flora while we were students, but I'm sure it's the right place. I remember thinking it looked odd from the outside, and number 43 is the only one that fits that description. It's a lone detached house on an otherwise terraced street, and so narrow that its detachedness looks like a mistake—as if it's been cut off the row as an afterthought and shoved along a bit. It protrudes awkwardly from the low-walled private garden that's been built around it like a little green island.

"Would you mind waiting in the car?" I ask Zannah.

"Yes."

"I think they'll tell me more if I'm alone. They know Flora and I were best friends for years. And confiding's easier to do with an audience of only one, I think."

"All right. If you insist. But remember everything they say. Even better, record it."

Recording a voice memo is one of the few things that my phone and I both know how to do. Dom showed me so that I could illicitly record Ben singing, with the most reluctance and embarrassment I've ever seen packed into one boy in a school hall, a song called "Piratical Style" from the musical *Pirates of the Curry Bean*.

"Wish me luck," I say to Zannah as I get out of the car. I'm not going to record Flora's parents if I'm lucky enough to find them—I'd feel guilty and it would show on my face—but Dom gave me some wise advice about a year ago, one day when I was crying because, yet again, Zannah and I were at loggerheads. He said: "Try this: say a direct 'No' as rarely as possible. If it's possible to not give in but not actually say, 'No, you can't' or 'No, I won't' then do it. It works like magic." I thought it sounded like the worst advice I'd ever heard, but I tried it and it worked.

I ring number 43's bell. The door is part glass, and through the leaded panes, I see a figure coming toward me along the hall. A tall man.

When he opens the door, I recognize him as Flora's dad, Gerard Tillotson. Ged, his wife used to call him. His hair is white now and he's thinner.

"Mr. Tillotson?" I say with a tentative smile.

"Hello? You're not going to try and sell me anything, are you? Because I'm not buying—not today! Haha! I don't need any more dishcloths or clothes pegs."

I wonder if my two-tone hair has made him think I must be a gypsy. "It's nothing like that," I say. "My name's Beth Leeson. Perhaps you remember me?"

"At my advanced age, I remember very little, my dear. Here's my advice to you: don't get old. There's really not much to recommend it."

"I was at university with . . ." I stop and clear my throat. "For a long time, I was best friends with Flora. Your daughter," I add unnecessarily. His memory might not be what it once was, but he's likely to remember his only child.

"Is Flora all right?" he says quickly.

"Um . . . yes, I . . . I'm not here with bad news or anything like that." As I say this, I wonder if it's true. What if Gerard Tillotson thinks everything in Flora's life is fine? Should I tell him that I don't think it is? Would that be fair?

"Ah. Well, that's a relief." He looks down at his right shoulder, as if trying to decide what to do. "I'm afraid Flora's not here, if you came in the hope of finding her," he says eventually.

"Oh—no, I know that. It's not that. I was hoping to speak to you, actually. And Mrs. Tillotson if she's around." *Shit*. I shouldn't have said that. Flora's mum might be dead for all I know. "It's quite important."

If it were my child, I'd want to know. Whatever anyone feared or suspected, I'd rather be told so that I could try and sort it out, however old I was.

Gerard Tillotson says, "If you walk around the house, you will find—unsurprisingly—the back garden. At the far end of it is a little blue-painted structure. It used to be a shed, but my wife spruced it up and now calls it the summer house. You'll find her inside it, surrounded by her dress-making equipment." He closes the door without a good-bye. Through the glass, I watch him walk back down the hall and disappear into a room.

What am I supposed to do now? Shouldn't he be the one to go and get his wife? Would he have told me where I'd find her if he didn't want me to seek her out?

I walk around the side of the house. The blue former shed is there, as described, at the end of a long, tapering back garden. There are white net curtains at its windows, with small orange and green flowers standing out like birthmarks, raising the skin of the gauzy fabric in lumps. I knock on the door and it opens immediately.

Rosemary Tillotson's hair is as white as her husband's. Unlike her husband, she is now heavier than she used to be. I see a large cream-colored sewing machine behind her, a patchwork rug on the floor, and some peach-colored fabric spread out on a table.

"Oh!" She smiles, as if I'm a rabbit that's popped out of a hat. "This is a surprise. Can I help you?"

"My name's Beth Leeson. I'm . . . I used to be Flora's best friend. You've met me before, ages ago."

"Flora's . . ." Her mouth moves, but nothing comes out. Then she looks past me, into her garden, and says, "Is Flora here?"

"No, she's not, though I've seen her a couple of times recently. I was hoping to talk to you and your husband about her, if that's okay."

Rosemary Tillotson frowns. "I'm not sure if it is. You can't just come here. You can't just . . ." I'm preparing to defend myself when the angry words stop and Flora's mother bursts into tears.

Twenty minutes later, Zannah and I are sitting in the Tillotsons' long, narrow, bay-windowed living room. The four of us are drinking tea from blue and white pottery mugs. I was in the car, ready to give up and drive back home, when Flora's father tapped on the window and inclined his head to indicate that I should come back to the house. Since he had seen Zannah, I decided it would be strange if I didn't bring her in with me.

"I'd better tell you, and I hope you don't take it personally, that your visit comes as rather a shock to us," he says now. "Foolishly, selfishly, quite reprehensibly, I decided that my wife would be better able to cope with the shock and to deal with *you* than I would be myself."

Rosemary Tillotson hasn't said a word to me since she had her crying fit. She's sitting by her husband's side on the sofa, red-eyed and mute. He has apologized four times so far for her distress, and I've apologized for causing it.

Something is very wrong here, and I wish I knew what it was—whether it's the same something-wrong as at Newnham House. Are Gerard and Rosemary Tillotson, at this moment, gearing up to lie to me as thoroughly as Kevin Cater and Fake Jeanette did?

So far, I've seen this living room, the hall and bottom of the stairs, the bathroom under the stairs and the kitchen. That's the entire ground floor of the house. There are no photographs of Flora, Lewis or their children anywhere to be seen. Unusual for grandparents. My mum has photos of Zannah and Ben at every age plastered all over her house.

"Perhaps you could tell us why you're here?" Gerard Tillotson asks.

I'd intended to tell them the whole story. That was before I knew that a visit from their daughter's former best friend would prove so traumatic for them. With Rosemary's blotchy face in front of me, I can't bring myself to say that I saw two of her grandchildren last Saturday and they didn't seem to have aged in twelve years. Before I reveal too much, I need to know why my turning up has made the Tillotsons so distraught.

"I wouldn't have come if I'd known it'd upset you," I say. "It's just that . . . when Flora and Lewis moved to Florida, they sold their house in Hemingford Abbots to a family called the Caters. I happened to drive past the house the other day, on my way to take my son to his football match, and I saw . . . well, I thought I saw Flora there, outside the house. And then I saw her again in Huntingdon and . . . the way she behaved made me worry that something was really wrong. I spoke to her briefly on the phone, and to Lewis, and they both said she wasn't in England. According to them, she's in Florida—which makes sense, because that's where they live now, but I know what I saw and I can't think—"

"Do they?" says Gerard. There's a sharp edge to his voice. "Does Flora live in America?"

"Are you saying she doesn't? Have she and Lewis split up? Is he in Florida, but she's still in England?"

Zannah coughs and fires a harsh look in my direction. She thinks I need to shut up and give the Tillotsons a chance to answer.

Gerard takes a sip of his tea. He looks at Rosemary, who doesn't notice. She seems unaware of her surroundings and of the conversation.

"We've had no contact with Flora since May 2007," he says. "Nor with Lewis or the children. We know nothing about a move to Florida, I'm afraid, nor about the condition of our daughter's marriage."

My head and heart start to spin. How can that be true? Flora was closer to her parents than anyone I've ever known. At university, she would ring them every night to say good night and tell them she loved them. She kept this up even after she married Lewis. He used to tease her about it.

"We don't google, and we don't inquire," says her father. "No doubt Lewis is taking the world by storm in one way or another—he always was destined for great things—but we prefer not to know anything about it. It would be too painful for us to have to contend with regular snippets of information. All our friends and acquaintances know that, if they happen to hear anything, we don't wish to be informed."

"Did you say May 2007?" I ask.

"That's right," says Gerard. "Lewis and Flora sat where you and your daughter are sitting now, and Lewis explained that we wouldn't be seeing or hearing from them, or from our grand-children, again. He meant it, too. Oh, we were in no doubt that he meant it."

My instincts are telling me that I need to get out of here and away, fast, so that I can think this through. I force myself to stay seated. Until last Saturday, the last time I saw Flora was in February 2007. Shortly before that, in December 2006, I felt betrayed by her for the first time in our long friendship. But what if . . . ?

I push the thought from my mind. If I get caught up in thinking it through now, I won't be able to concentrate on the Tillotsons.

"Why?" I ask. "Sorry, I don't mean . . . I understand why you don't want to hear any news and how upsetting that would be, but why aren't you in touch with Flora? The Flora I knew—"

"Might as well have died," says Rosemary Tillotson suddenly. "Afterward, she wasn't the same person. She wasn't our lovely, happy daughter. She was a stranger."

"Afterward?"

Rosemary nods.

"She means after Georgina died," says Gerard.

Oh, God, please, no. No, no, no. The room spins around me. For a few seconds, I can't breathe. All the air is stopped solid in my lungs.

"Mum, are you okay?" Zannah asks.

"Georgina died?" I say, once I'm able to speak. "How? When?"

"April the twenty-seventh, 2007. She was six months old. She just . . . stopped breathing."

"Cot death?" I say.

"Sudden Infant Death Syndrome, I believe they call it. Georgina wasn't the strongest baby to begin with. There were various complications. She was born six weeks premature, and there was something wrong with her right eye. She would have needed surgery to correct it at some point, or perhaps an eye patch would have done the trick. She wasn't as robust as both Thomas and Emily were as babies."

"Flora didn't . . ." *Of course she didn't tell you, idiot. She didn't tell you any of it. Don't you remember the sequence of events?*

"She stopped being Flora," says Rosemary. "The old Flora—the *real* Flora—would never have cut us off. Never. We'd done nothing wrong, nothing at all."

"Which of course is what parents who deserve to be ostracized would say," her husband adds. "But we didn't deserve it. Not a bit."

Then why? Why did it happen?

I can't bring myself to ask them if, before she died, Georgina's nickname was Chimpy. It probably makes no sense that I still have the urge to ask this question. If Georgina is dead, how could Flora have been talking to her on the phone last Saturday?

"Would you like a hanky or a tissue?" Rosemary asks me.

"No, thank you." I sniff and wipe my eyes quickly with the back of my hand.

She says, "When Flora and Lewis told us that Georgina had died, I looked at Flora and I knew right away: she was gone. As gone as Georgina was. Somebody else was there instead. A different woman."

"We only saw them twice after Georgina's death," says Gerard. "Once when they told us the terrible news and the second time when Lewis said we would never see them again and that we mustn't try to contact them."

"But why would Flora want that?" I blurt out. "You say she'd changed—anyone would change after a tragedy like that, but to push away your own parents . . ."

"Please." Gerard raises a hand. He's telling me, as politely as he can, to shut up. "All the questions you're likely to ask are ones we asked ourselves, again and again. We didn't understand. Of course we didn't. After such a tragedy, to be bereaved again so unnecessarily—and if you think it's too dramatic to call being cut off by your daughter and remaining grandchildren a bereavement, I can assure you, that's exactly how it felt and how it still feels."

"I can imagine," I say shakily.

But it can't have been Flora's fault. None of it can. She'd never have cut you off if she'd had a choice.

How the hell am I going to manage the long drive home after this?

Gerard says, "Since I'm no longer in touch with Flora, I obviously can't ask her why she made the decision that she made. I have my suspicions, if you'd like to hear them?"

"Only if you don't mind telling us," says Zannah.

Thank you, Zan. Thanks for speaking when I can't. If Zannah or Ben ever cut off contact with me, I'd throw myself off a bridge there and then. I wouldn't try to be brave for anyone else's sake. I couldn't live in a world where my daughter didn't want to know me.

Gerard says, "I think . . . well, I *know*, from my own experience, that most people will go to extraordinary lengths to avoid unbearable pain. It's what we've done since losing Flora and the children. It's the reason your visit, and your mention of Flora's name, caused us such, uh, consternation, shall we say? Flora and Lewis knew that every time they saw us, every interaction they had with us in the future, they would have to confront *our* loss, the grief that *we* felt at losing Georgina. I don't think they could face that prospect. I must say, it doesn't surprise me to hear that they've moved to America. It fits with my suspicion: they want to surround themselves with people who have no memories of Georgina. It will make life easier for them. Perhaps it's the only way they can face living at all."

People who have no memories of Georgina . . . Not me, then. I remember Georgina very clearly, from her one visit to my house. Even if I'd never met her in person, there was no chance I would ever forget her.

Thoughts and memories crash-land in my mind, one after another: Flora on the phone, ending the call as soon as she could, promising to ring back and then not ringing back. Flora running away from me in a Huntingdon car park, Lewis on the phone from Delray Beach, Florida—happy to chat at length, confident he could sustain his lies for as long as I could keep him talking.

Flora wasn't confident or happy to talk, though she did her best to pretend to be. She could only stretch out her lies for a finite amount of time. And then she couldn't risk ringing back. When she saw me in the car park in Huntingdon, she didn't brazen it out, as Lewis would no doubt have done. She turned and ran.

She was scared. *Of me*. Shit, how can this not have struck me before? She was on her way back to her car, presumably strolling along in a reasonably normal frame of mind, and then she saw me and she freaked out. Ran away. I was the thing that caused that rush of fear—because she knew I'd ask after Georgina and she didn't want to have to talk about her death? But . . .

No. That can't be it. You might try and avoid an old friend in those circumstances, but the fear I saw in Flora's eyes, the way she turned and ran . . . that wasn't just reluctance to talk about a past tragedy. It was more and bigger than that. And then, to send that other woman back to the car park wearing her clothes . . .

"I'm worried Flora's in danger," I say before I can stop myself. "I'm not sure I can explain it very well, but . . . Flora and Lewis both lied to me. The people living in their old house lied. There are no pictures of Flora on Lewis's Instagram page—only of him, Thomas and Emily. I know none of this proves she's in danger, but I think something is really wrong."

"Beth, please try to understand," says Gerard. "We can't help you. We don't know the answers to any questions you might ask. You know more than we do, and I'm afraid that conversations like this one won't do me or my wife any good at all. It's going to take us weeks, possibly months, to recover from your visit. Nothing you've said suggests danger to me so much as . . . well, hard though this might be for you to hear, I think it sounds as if Flora and Lewis don't want you in their life anymore—much the same way they felt about us."

"But they told you quite directly, didn't they? That's not what they're doing with me."

"Mum, we should go," Zannah says quietly.

"I'm sorry. Sorry to be so . . . relentless. Can I ask you one more question before I leave?"

"I'd rather you didn't," says Gerard, at the same time that Rosemary says, "Yes."

"Did you like Lewis? Were you happy to have him as a son-in-law? Did you ever worry that he might . . ." I can't bring myself to say it.

"Harm Flora?" says Rosemary. "No. Never. He adored Flora and the children. Treated them as if they were made of gold. I didn't like him, though."

Gerard makes a spluttering noise. He puts down his cup of tea and wipes his mouth. "Rosemary, of course you liked Lewis. We both did."

"I didn't."

"You did," he insists, looking perplexed.

"I pretended to. I've always pretended to, even after they told us they didn't want us in their lives anymore. It was probably silly of me, Ged. You and I should have discussed it before now. I shouldn't have told you in front of people we hardly know."

"Never mind," he says. He looks as if he does, though.

"Why didn't you like him?" I ask Rosemary.

"It's hard to describe, especially at a distance of so many years. But whenever he came here, I felt as if I was a guest in *his* house and not the other way around. Not even a guest, actually. More of a servant. He always had an air of being in charge, even in places where he shouldn't have been. Even in my kitchen."

"He was always perfectly genial, as far as I recall," Gerard defends the man who told him he'd never see his daughter or grandchildren again. "Life and soul of every gathering."

"But we couldn't be ourselves around him, Ged. Not at all."

"I could."

"Well, I couldn't," says Rosemary in a shaky voice. "I always felt I needed to please and impress him, and that, if I didn't, my relationship with Flora would suffer. I worked out, very early on, what kind of mother-in-law he would most want, and then I pretended to be that person."

"When I spoke to Lewis on the phone, I asked after Georgina," I tell her. "I said, 'How old is she now?' Obviously, I had no idea she'd passed away. I said it in a 'Wow, she must be nearly a teenager' kind of way."

"Lewis won't have liked that *at all*," says Gerard Tillotson quietly. Something chimes at the back of my mind—some sort of alarm or warning—but it's gone before I can grasp it.

"What did he say?" asks Rosemary.

"He told me Georgina was twelve," I say. I know I've said enough, but I'm so furious with Lewis that I can't control it, and the rest spills out: "There was no hint of distress or unease in his voice. He sounded his usual, upbeat, extrovert self, even though, it turns out, he was telling me the most outrageous lie: that his daughter who died when she was six months old is alive and well and living in Delray Beach, Florida."

12

"Beth? It's pitch black in here," Dom complains.

I'm in the bath, in the dark, with Kiehl's Lavender, Sea Salts and Aloe Vera bath foam and a few extra drops of essential lavender oil added for good measure, to make the scent stronger. My face is covered with a stiff, dried mask: Zannah's favorite—a blend of lavender and chamomile that comes as a powder. You have to add water and stir it into a paste.

Some people believe that tea is the answer to stress, and others resort to alcohol. For me, it's lavender.

"You want to talk yet?" says Dom.

I nod. I'm ready. It might be nearly midnight, but since getting back from Wokingham I've dealt with my work email inbox and had an hour or so to get my thoughts in order. The bath has helped hugely. I feel like I have a grip on things again. I've adjusted, digested all the new information.

"Good." Dom closes the door and locks it. Now we're in total darkness.

"Can I turn a light on?" he asks.

"No. Your eyes'll adjust in a minute."

He sits down on the floor, leaning his back against the wall. "We need to talk," he says. "Seriously."

"I agree."

"Great. I'm glad."

I know what's coming.

"You need to drop this now. Completely. No more driving to

far-away places, no more hanging around schools. And don't turn this into 'My husband doesn't understand my point of view,' because that's not true. I do."

"I've literally never said those words, by the way."

"Zan told me what happened at Flora's parents' place. Something fucked up is going on with Lewis and Flora, big time, but it doesn't affect us. By which I mean: it doesn't need to, unless you keep your obsession stoked up. You've been lied to and fobbed off repeatedly—that means Flora and Lewis don't want you to know what's going on with them, they want you out of their lives. Let that happen—stop pursuing this—and we'll never see or hear from the Braids again. And that'll be *brilliant*, Beth. That'll be the best possible outcome."

"For who?"

"All of us. Me, you, Zan and Ben."

"And we're the only people who matter?"

"In this case, yes. No one's having their life threatened or endangered, are they? Flora's walking around, going about her normal business. She seems not to be in too terrible a state, apart from when she sees you stalking her."

"I'm not—"

"So you heard her talking on the phone outside her house and she sounded upset—so what? These people haven't been our friends for *twelve years*. Let them get on with their lives, whatever weirdness those lives might involve, and let's us get on with ours. The alternative is what? Letting down more clients? Isn't that going to harm your business? You've always been the one out of the two of us who cares about your job. Maybe you don't anymore, but it's not only about you."

Here it comes.

"Today, Zannah should have been at home revising. Instead, she was sticking her nose into other people's business and getting drunk. That can't happen again, Beth."

"I agree. It was a one-off."

"Yeah, well, it should have been a none-off." He sounds slightly mollified.

"I've made a decision. I need one more day, and then I'll stop. At that point I'll have done all I can. I've already rescheduled all the clients I canceled. They're all fine about it. Zannah's got some revision sessions coming up at school, which she'll go to. Our lives aren't falling apart, Dom. We're all fine."

"Right, and we're going to stay fine—by accepting that other people's lives are their business and their problem. I don't agree that you need one more day."

I don't care.

"What will this extra day involve?"

"I'm going to go to Huntingdon and try and talk to the police there."

"What?" Dom laughs. "Beth, no crime has been committed."

"I agree, there's no proof of any crime."

"But you think there is one?"

"I've no way of knowing, and no power to find out. I strongly suspect something is really horribly wrong. For all I know, it involves an element of crime. Generally, people don't go to such extreme lengths to hide whatever they're hiding unless it's criminal. One person alone might be desperate to hide a shameful personal secret, but four? Lewis, Flora, Kevin Cater and the woman who told us she was Jeanette?"

"Yeah, they're four liars who all know each other. It's hardly a huge underground network. And there's absolutely no reason to suspect a criminal conspiracy. But . . . you're not going to take my word for it, so let's go and see the police. Maybe if you hear them say, 'We don't think there's anything for us to investigate here,' it'll put your mind at rest."

"It won't stop me wondering what's going on. I don't think anything could, apart from finding out the answer. But I need to know that I've done everything I possibly could to help Flora and . . . whoever those two kids were that I saw outside her house. And the two in Florida. All of them."

"You said the two kids you saw outside the Wyddial Lane house last Saturday looked normal and healthy," says Dom.

"They did."

"And it's clear from Lewis's Instagram that Thomas and Emily are doing great. So there's no evidence that anyone's harming any kids, is there?"

"Dom, for God's sake."

"What? What did I say?"

I sit up and wash off the face mask. Once it's all gone, I say, "How sure are you that those four children are fine—the two in England and the two in America? Really think about it, Dom. I heard Flora call the two little ones Thomas and Emily. They were outside Kevin Cater's house, and Lou Munday at Kimbolton Prep School told me that those are the Cater kids' names: Thomas and Emily. That means it's likely to be them that I saw."

"I know all this."

"The two kids I saw were absolutely beyond a shadow of a doubt Flora's children. Like teenage Thomas and Emily when they were little, they bore a strikingly strong resemblance to Flora. There's no way they aren't hers. So. Think about what that means."

Dom stands up. He walks over to the bathroom mirror and stares at himself. Eventually he says, "Flora had three children. One died. Then she had two more and called them the same names as the two children she already had."

"Except no one does that," I say.

"But *she* has." Dom turns to face me. He looks confused. "If everything you've just said is true, that the younger two must be Flora's, then that must be what happened."

"Must it? We've only seen pictures of teenage Thomas and Emily on the Internet. The people in those pictures could be actors hired by Lewis."

Dom snorts. "Beth. Come on, get a grip."

"What? You think that's implausible? He pretended Flora was in Florida when she was in Cambridgeshire. He told me Georgina's twelve. She's not twelve—she's dead."

"Is she? If Lewis can lie so easily, maybe Georgina's alive. Maybe she's Chimpy, and you heard Flora talking to her on Saturday."

"Maybe I did." I've been thinking this myself. "All the options we've considered, all the ones we can possibly think of, are worrying, aren't they? Let's say all five kids are alive, but Lewis and Flora are telling Georgina's grandparents that she's dead. Or Georgina's two younger siblings have the same Christian names as her two older ones, and meanwhile their parents are telling weird lies and enlisting their friends to do the same. Does any of that sound to you like a family in which the kids definitely aren't at risk from the adults? Because it sure as fuck doesn't to me. I want to say all this to the police. I think there's something sinister going on that needs looking into."

"Unless . . ." I can tell from this halfhearted start that Dom knows the point he's about to make is a weak one. "My friend Anthony at university had the same first name as all his brothers: John. They were all known by their middle names, but—"

"Great. You can tell Huntingdon police that. I'll tell them Flora's two youngest kids are known by the names Thomas and Emily, which is what I heard her call them—the same names her first two were known by."

"Shouldn't you also be contacting the police in Delray Beach, Florida, if you think the original Thomas and Emily might also be at risk?"

"Huntingdon police can do that, assuming they agree with me."

"Christ, Beth." Dom covers his face with his hands. "Is that what you're hoping will happen? It won't. The police aren't going to lift a finger, however weird it all is. The most they'll do is send in social services."

"Fine. That's good enough for me."

Liar.

No matter what I tell Dom, nothing will be good enough for me unless and until I have the answers I need.

I say, "Flora's dad said that she and Lewis probably don't want anything to do with me now, just like they don't want Flora's parents in their lives anymore. If that were true, if that's all that's happening here, why wouldn't Lewis have said so on the phone? He was very direct when he cut off Flora's parents. Why not say to me, 'Sorry, Beth, we've moved on, you're pretty much a stranger now, we don't have to answer any of your questions, good-bye'? Why would it be any harder to say that to me than to Gerard and Rosemary?"

"It wouldn't. But a more diplomatic brush-off is always easier, and most friends would take the hint. Whereas parents need to be told more firmly. They don't let their kids go so easily."

"Maybe. But Flora's reaction in the car park was hardly diplomatic. There was no 'Oh, Beth, how lovely to see you after all these years—must dash now but let's catch up sometime.' Running away in terror is pretty undiplomatic."

"True," Dom concedes.

"And Lewis telling us we must come to Florida, and Kevin Cater inviting us around to his house, answering our questions . . . Showing us that picture of two kids I'd never seen before, lying about Thomas and Emily's names. He could have given us a polite version of, 'I'm sorry, I've no idea what your wife is on about. Now please leave me alone.' Do you want to know what I think?"

Dom sighs heavily. "Beth, I do, but . . . this has to *end*. For us, our being part of it."

"I know. I know it does. I just . . ." I close my eyes and inhale deeply. *Come on, lavender. Work your magic.* "This isn't a criticism, but I don't understand how you're not as curious as I am. Don't you want to understand it, whatever it is?"

"Not at the expense of our lives, no. Also, to an extent, I think I already do understand it. Not the finer details, maybe, but the more general explanation 'Lewis Braid is a massive weirdo' works for me. And I really don't believe anyone's in danger, Beth. I think Lewis is bizarre enough to have invented some mad reason to call his youngest kids after his oldest kids."

"Why did Flora run away from me?" I stand up, grab a towel and wrap it around me. I was planning to wash my hair, but the plan had a built-in loophole: that I knew I wouldn't bother in the end. I hate washing my hair. It's the annoying chore that looms in the shadows at the end of every nice long bath, potentially ruining it.

"I don't know why Flora ran away." Dom sighs.

"To avoid talking to me, clearly. But why? She must have been scared I'd ask something or scared to tell me something, scared I'd find out whatever the secret is. Maybe she thought I'd found out already, maybe Marilyn Oxley told her I'd been asking about the Caters and Thomas and Emily. If the secret is something eccentric but harmless, her fear makes no sense."

"Maybe she was scared of you. Just you. Nothing to do with her secret."

My heart twists. *He can't know.*

"Why would she be?"

"I don't know. You tell me."

I turn away. I wish I could be indignant, but I can't. I've wondered the same thing myself. Though if Flora's scared of me because of what I did twelve years ago, that would be an absurd overreaction. She can't imagine that I'd . . .

"Beth, I'm sorry." Dom's voice cuts into my thoughts. "That was below the belt. There's nothing scary about you."

We all have things we'd rather people didn't find out about us. I don't want to, though. Not anymore. "I need to show you something," I say.

Dominic and I sit on opposite sides of our bed. Between us, lying on the duvet, is a cream envelope that I've dug out of an old handbag. The handwriting on the envelope is Flora's.

I couldn't bring myself to throw it away. Not at the time, and not at any point since. "Don't tell Zannah and Ben," I say. "I'm not proud of this and I'd rather they didn't know."

Dom nods.

I pick up the envelope and shake its contents out onto the bed: a Christmas card with a picture of Santa Claus and his reindeers flying over a snowy mountain. And a photograph of the Braids, with a slit that's been cut into it and a hole in the middle, where a small part's been excised . . . and then, lying a few inches apart from the other two items, the cutting from the picture, the person whose absence has made the hole: a tiny baby wrapped in a pink and white blanket, eyes closed. *Georgina Braid.*

I pick up the card and show Dom what's written inside it: "To Dom, Beth, Zannah and Ben, Merry Christmas and a Happy New Year! Lots of love from Lewis, Flora, Thomas, Emily and Georgina." Followed by three kisses, as per Braid family card-writing tradition. A perfectly ordinary message.

Georgina was two months old in the photograph. The last time the Braids came to visit us was February 2007, when Georgina was four months old, and two months before she died.

If she died.

Flora and I both knew that our friendship was over in February 2007, but we were pretending otherwise, to ourselves and to each other. Dominic had no idea. I don't know what Lewis knew or didn't know. I made a special fuss of baby Georgina, aware that not long ago I'd deliberately taken a pair of scissors and cut her out of a happy family photograph.

"Not my proudest moment," I say to Dom.

"You? Oh. I thought you were going to say that this was how it arrived—with Georgina cut out."

"No. I did it."

"Why?"

I remember as if it happened earlier today, though it was twelve years ago: once removed from the photograph, Georgina landed on the kitchen floor. Seeing her lying there, so tiny and separated from her family, I felt immediately ashamed. What the hell was I doing? What if cutting a child out of a family photo was like sticking pins in a wax model of someone you hated? I would always be someone who had done that to a baby. I could never undo it, which made me feel weirdly doomed—as if, with one vicious, unjustifiable act, I had sealed my fate.

That was my immediate reaction. Overreaction. A few minutes later I realized that all I'd done was cut up a photo, and what did it matter, really? Impulse control had never been my strong point and I knew I'd behaved pathetically, but it was hardly likely to harm Georgina Braid in real life.

Still, I couldn't bring myself to throw the Braids in the bin, after what I'd done already. I put the card and the pieces of the photograph back in the envelope, which I stuffed into the side pocket of my handbag. I told myself everything was fine, that no one would ever find out I'd done something so petty and spiteful.

"Flora found out," I tell Dom. It's a relief to say it out loud.

The horrible thing I'd done, and how bad it made me feel, was nothing compared with the shame I felt when Flora saw the evidence. Most people successfully hide the worst aspects of their characters from everyone they know, all their lives. I was unlucky.

"She found out you cut Georgina out of the photo she sent you? Jesus, Beth. I don't understand. At all."

"When the Braids came around for the last time . . . You probably won't remember, but you and Lewis went out to the Granta for a pint."

Dom shakes his head. Of course he doesn't remember.

"I knew Flora was thinking the same as me: we both wished you hadn't gone and left us alone—well, alone with the kids. We were chatting, trying to pretend everything was okay, but deep down we both knew it hadn't been normal for a while between us, and then suddenly Thomas started wailing. He'd pulled the skin off a blister on his heel and it was bleeding. Flora handed Georgina to me and started rummaging around in her changing bag, looking for a plaster. She didn't have one, but I knew I had one in my bag. I totally forgot, in that moment, that the cut-up picture was also in there. I sent Zan to look for the plaster. A few minutes later, back she came with all of that." I nod down at the photo pieces and the card. "She gave it to Flora and said, 'Look. This was in Mummy's bag. Someone's torn baby Georgina out of the photo.' She had no idea what she was doing, obviously. She just thought it was a weird thing she'd found, and that we'd want to know about it. I could feel myself turning bright red. One look at my face told Flora who the guilty party was."

Dom looks appalled, understandably. "Why the hell did you keep it? Why not chuck it in the rubbish once you've gone as far as cutting it up? What did Flora say? Anyone cut one of our kids out of a photograph, I'd punch their lights out."

"I didn't give her a chance to say anything. I started talking at a million miles an hour—saying how sorry I was, that I didn't know what had come over me. She was upset, but she said she understood. I explained how angry I'd been—that she'd not told me, and then sent the card and the photo, assuming I knew. She apologized for forgetting to tell me. She cried. It was a bit of an apology fest all around . . . and we both knew that was it, that we'd never see or speak to each other again."

"Jealousy," Dom says. "That was what came over you. Understandably, I suppose."

"What? No. You mean the miscarriage?" I try to fight the feeling of disappointment that's rising inside me. Dom's bound to think this. What else would he think? How can he know what I've never told him?

"Me losing a pregnancy had nothing to do with it," I say. "You might not believe that, but it's true."

"Then why the hell did you cut a baby out of a photo?"

"Because Flora never told me about her, and I was . . . more hurt than you can probably imagine. When she got pregnant with Thomas, she told me right away. When I knew I was pregnant with Zannah, I rang Flora within ten minutes of taking the test. I think I told her before I told you. You were in a meeting and I couldn't get hold of you . . ."

Dom waves impatiently to indicate that he doesn't care about not being told first.

"When we both got pregnant a second time, same thing: Flora phoned me immediately after she'd told Lewis and her mum. I phoned her within an hour of knowing I was pregnant with Ben. With my third pregnancy, it was different. I told Flora because I always had before, not because I really wanted to. Lewis had inherited his fortune by then, and . . . I don't know if it was us or them, but somehow the idea of this huge wealth that they suddenly had came between us."

"Did it?"

"I didn't talk to you about it because I wanted to pretend it wasn't happening. You didn't notice or care, because Lewis never mattered to you the way Flora mattered to me. But we saw them a bit less, and it was awkward when we did see them. And I thought it had to be the money that had made things different, but . . . thinking about it now, the change happened at the same time that Flora must have found out she was pregnant with Georgina. Oh, God, Dom, I've been such a terrible friend."

"You mean cutting up the photo?"

"Not only that." I blink back tears. "I used to think that defacing a happy family photo like a psycho was the worst thing I'd done. Not anymore."

"Beth, what are you talking about?"

"I'm trying to tell you!"

"Sorry. Go on."

"When I had the miscarriage, I had to tell everyone who knew I'd been pregnant. Including Flora. She was really nice on the phone. Sympathetic. I thought, 'Maybe we'll be okay, maybe the awkwardness between us was just a blip and now things'll go back to normal.' We talked about meeting up and she said she'd ring me to arrange something, but she never did. We didn't see or hear from her or Lewis at all, for months. It was like they'd forgotten us completely. And then, just before Christmas, *those* arrived." I nod at the card and photo pieces.

"You mean . . . ?"

"Yep. Flora had been pregnant and had a baby *and not told me*. Not the day she found out, like she had with Thomas and Emily, and not ever. She went through an entire pregnancy and birth without telling me. I had no idea. And then suddenly, just before Christmas, a card arrives signed from all of them, including Georgina, and there's the photo of the five of them and . . . it's as if Flora's forgotten, or doesn't care enough to be aware of it, that she's had another baby and told me nothing about it. That's how I found out. From being sent *that*." I point to the evidence: evidence of Flora's awful behavior as well as mine.

"I called her. Soon as I'd finished crying, cutting up the photo, hiding what I'd done—inadequately, as it turned out—I called Flora. She sounded normal. Well, normal for New Rich Flora. I thought, 'She has no idea why I'm calling.' I said, 'I got your Christmas card. Flora, I didn't know you'd had another baby. I didn't even know you were pregnant.'"

"What did she say?"

"She sounded puzzled at first. She said, 'Didn't you? You must have known!' Then there was this long, horrible silence, during which she must have realized I couldn't have known because she never told me. She's not stupid, and she knows I'm not either. We both knew that any charade of us still being best friends was finished."

"Maybe she didn't tell you because of the miscarriage," Dom says. "She didn't want to rub salt into the wound."

"No. There was no planning or strategy. If she'd thought about it, she'd have known that for me to find out in the way I did would be the most hurtful thing of all. She just wasn't thinking about me at all. At the time, I thought it was because she didn't give a shit about me anymore."

"But . . . if this phone call revealed that the two of you weren't close friends anymore, how did they end up coming around to ours with Georgina?"

"After that conversation, Flora briefly felt bad enough to make a bit of an effort. And I wanted to believe the friendship could still recover. But from the second they arrived, things were wrong and awkward and . . . bad. I assumed it was because Flora felt so guilty about not having told me, or maybe she didn't want to be there and was just doing a duty visit, for form's sake. I was wrong."

"How?"

"I'm scared you'll think I'm a terrible person if I tell you," I say tearfully. "I'm scared I *am* a terrible person."

"Don't be silly. Just tell me."

"All these years, I've been making it all about me. When Flora changed and seemed less interested in me, I put it down to Lewis's inheritance. When months passed and I didn't hear from her, it never once occurred to me that she might be in trouble. When she was pregnant and had a baby and didn't tell me, I used it to back up my theory: that she and Lewis were rich now so she didn't need to bother with the likes of me anymore. I didn't ever think, 'Flora wouldn't treat me like this unless something was really wrong.' And I should have thought that, Dom—because she wouldn't."

Finally, Dom sees what I'm driving at: "You think that whatever weird shit's going on now started then?"

"Yes, I do. And . . . after that last time they came to ours, I drew the wrong conclusion again. Apart from their new address card, Flora never contacted me after the day she found out I'd cut up the photo. I assumed that was why . . . but it wasn't. Sure, she'd have been hurt by that, but it wasn't the reason. Flora never got in touch again because she couldn't risk having me in her life anymore. She couldn't risk being close to me—because if she was then I might find out the truth. The secret. Whatever that was. Is," I correct myself. "Dom, whatever it is, *it started before Georgina was born*. Months before."

"I wish we'd talked about this at the time. I had no idea—about any of it."

"I didn't want to talk about it. I was . . . ashamed, I guess.

People aren't supposed to feel jilted and have their hearts broken by their friends."

Sudden ringing makes me jump. "Is that your phone?" Dom asks.

I nod, reaching down to pull my handbag up onto the bed.

"Who'd call this late at night?"

My heart judders as I look at the screen. "It's Lewis," I say, recognizing the number I tried to call back so many times on Sunday evening.

"Answer it."

"Hello? Lewis? Hello?"

I hear muffled noise in the background. Movement.

"Is anyone there? Lewis?"

"Beth?"

"Who is this?"

"I meant to ring you back the other night, and then life took over and I never did. I'm sorry."

"Flora?"

"Hi, Beth! Say hi to Rom-com Dom from me!" Lewis Braid calls out in the background.

"Yes, it's me," Flora says. "Beth? Can you hear me okay?"

I can. It's definitely her. Definitely him, too; no one else calls my husband Rom-com Dom. It's Lewis and Flora Braid. In Florida, now. Together.

If you keep turning up outside someone's house, and lie about why when they ask what you're doing there . . . well, it looks as if you might be an obsessive stalker, doesn't it?"

"So?"

She's impatient for the conclusion, but I'm not quite there yet. "Lewis Braid is the father of Thomas and Emily Cater. They have his eyes, just like older Thomas and Emily do. Flora was with him when she rang me last week. That means he's still around, still involved in whatever's going on at Newnham House." I raise my hand to stop Zannah asking questions before I've finished. "But he's not supposed to be. Think about the lies he and Flora have told me: Georgina's twelve and doing great; they have no young children, only the three they had when they moved to America, where they now live; they have no connection with Hemingford Abbots anymore."

"I don't get it, Mum."

"Tilly kept finding Lewis loitering outside her house. Then she found him in her back garden clutching her silk pajamas, at which point he declared his obsessive love for her. She and her husband had a word with him, he promised faithfully to stop, and he did—he never bothered them again."

"Uh-huh."

"Stalkers don't just stop, Zan. Someone as determined and driven as Lewis Braid wouldn't have given up so easily. Nor would he pick Tilly to obsess over. She isn't his type. So why would he pretend to stalk her and be in love with her?"

"I don't think he would," says Zannah. "You can't be sure—"

"I'm sure," I cut her off. "Think about what Tilly told us: the pajamas in the back garden and the crying and admitting it all—that came later. The first thing, she said, was that she noticed Lewis outside her house a few times. I assumed she meant he was lurking in her front garden near the house—number 3 doesn't have any gates, so that's possible—but she didn't say that. She said 'outside my house.' That could mean that *she* was in her front garden or on her driveway and she saw Lewis in his car, parked where we parked when we went to Wyddial Lane."

"If she just saw him in a car on the street, she wouldn't assume he was in love with her." Zan rolls her eyes.

"No, but if she spotted him more than once, she might think, 'Why does he keep turning up? I thought the Braids had moved to America.' And think about what kind of person Tilly is. She said the first few times she confronted Lewis, he made crap excuses for being there. That probably means she trotted enthusiastically up to his car, knocked on the window, said, 'Hi, Lewis! What are you doing back? I thought you'd moved to America.' And he was forced to lie."

"I've been to Wyddial Lane three times now. It's a silent, mind-your-own-business sort of place. Everyone's hiding behind their high walls and gates, not watching what's happening on the road. I'd bet everything I own that no one except Tilly on that street would rush up to a parked car and cheerfully demand to know the business of the person sitting inside it. Marilyn Oxley at number 14 is nosy and observant enough, but she's also keen on keeping her distance. You should have seen the effort I had to put in to persuade her to leave her house and come and talk to me through the gate. Anyone would have thought I was waving a bomb around or something."

"Okay, so Tilly saw Lewis parked outside her house, and she went and tried to chat to him," says Zannah. "She asked him what he was doing there, and he made crap excuses. I still don't get it."

Silvia picks this moment to wander over to our table. "You ladies want more rolls? More coffee?"

"No thanks," I say.

"They are very good, though?"

"Sublime, as always."

"Ah, you are very kind to me!" She wanders away. Mercifully, there's been no singing so far today.

I say to Zannah, "Lewis would have known his excuses for being there weren't remotely plausible. That will have bothered him. He'll have worried that he'd made Tilly suspicious. If the lie that he and Flora desperately want the world to believe is that they're living in Florida, done with Wyddial Lane, and a different family now owns their old house, a family that has nothing to do with them—"

"I get it!" Zannah flaps her hands. "So he starts acting like *more* of a stalker to Tilly and gets caught with her PJs in the garden deliberately."

"Yes. If he arranges it so that she 'finds out'"—I make air quotes with my fingers—"that he's been stalking her, and then breaks down and sobs and says he loves her wildly, then his crap excuses are no longer suspicious. Suddenly, there's an explanation that looks obvious."

"And it explains why he then stopped stalking her: because he never wanted to or really did in the first place. Wait: that only works if you're right about Tilly first spotting him in his car on the street, not in her garden."

"I'm going to contact her and find out," I say. "I didn't take her number, but I know she runs a business from 3 Wyddial Lane. Shouldn't be hard to find."

"Another thing I just thought of," Zan says. "You know what Tilly said about none of the neighbors ever seeing Flora? What if that was deliberate? Lewis and Flora planned it so that no one saw her because they knew she'd be coming back as Jeanette Cater. They didn't want the neighbors to say, 'Wait, you're not Jeanette, you're Flora.'"

A shiver runs through my body. Pretending to be an obsessive stalker, hiding from the world so that you can come back with a different name . . . What can the Braids be so determined to hide that they'd go to such extremes? The more I know about the lengths they've gone to, the more convinced I am that the truth must be unbearable. For who, though? The Braids themselves, or for other people?

"Did Georgina Braid have Lewis's eyes like the other four?" Zannah asks.

"I don't know. Don't think I ever saw her with her eyes open. She was a tiny baby the only time they came around. Resemblances often don't become obvious till you're a bit older, anyway." Even in the photograph Flora sent with the Christmas card, Georgina had her eyes shut. The image of that tiny cutting lying on my kitchen floor flashes up in my mind. I push it away. "Why?" I ask Zannah.

"Dunno. I just wondered if she might have been Kevin and Yanina's baby, not Lewis and Flora's." Zannah laughs at my immediately alert expression. "Relax, Mum. That's not a brilliant new theory. I don't know why I said it."

"You wouldn't have said it for no reason." If Flora was never pregnant with Georgina, then what I was annoyed about never happened: she didn't fail to tell me that she was pregnant or that she'd had a baby—because she wasn't, and she didn't.

Zannah says, "Assuming you're right about the eyes thing . . . which, okay, I believe you. Then little Thomas and Emily are Lewis and Flora's, but everyone's pretending they're Kevin and Jeanette Cater's. But there is no Jeanette Cater, not really, and Yanina lives in that house too, and she and Kevin might be together . . ."

"And also might not be."

"It would be neat, though," Zan says. "A straight swap. Kevin and Yanina have Georgina and for some reason Flora and Lewis pretend she's theirs. Then a few years later, Lewis and Flora have Thomas and Emily number two, and Kevin pretends they're his."

None of this strikes me as impossible or even unlikely, given all that's happened and everything I know to be true. It would explain why Flora seemed distant and less interested in spending time with me in 2006, when she—or somebody—was pregnant with Georgina. If she knew she was about to have to tell the world the most outrageous lie and then sustain it, pretending that another woman's baby was hers, there wouldn't have been room in her mind or life for anything else. And . . . she wouldn't have wanted her parents around her, either. They knew her better than anyone; they'd have been able to tell for sure that she wasn't herself, that something was horribly wrong.

I was too wrapped up in what I thought was her rejection of me to worry about what might have been going on in her life. It's unbearable to think that Thomas and Emily Cater might be suffering now because of my failure to realize twelve years ago that not everything was about me.

Flora's suffering is more complicated. She has to be one of the main liars behind all this, whatever it is, but I've twice seen her behave like a victim.

"That could be what 'Chimpy' means, if Chimpy's Georgina," Zannah goes on. "Lewis and Flora and their kids are all perfect looking, aren't they? Kevin and Yanina's kid might not have been. From what you've said about Lewis, I can imagine him giving someone an insulting nickname, and expecting them to find it funny."

"Taunting," I mutter.

"What?" says Zan.

"You're right. Lewis liked to taunt people with nicknames, so you might be right about Chimpy. But what if he took it further?"

"How?"

"If you call your youngest two children names that your oldest two already have, and make them wear their old clothes and shoes . . . Couldn't there be an element of taunting there too?"

"That's creepy, Mum."

It is. And if it's not true, if it's miles away from the truth, then maybe I'm the sick one for dreaming it up. Flora would never willingly harm a child, especially not her own.

Lewis is a different matter. I have no idea what he's capable of, and I can't help asking myself the question: what if he chose to call his youngest children Thomas and Emily as a deliberate act of cruelty?

Dom's hovering in the hall when Zannah and I get home. "PC Pollard rang," he says, trying to sound matter-of-fact. In the short silence that follows, I hear the gloating he's trying so hard not to indulge in: *I told you he would.*

I drop my bag on the floor—something I frequently moan at the children for doing. "What did he say?"

"Tell me about school first."

"It's all fine. Sorted out."

"I was hoping for a bit more detail than that." Seeing my glare, Dom says, "Pollard went to 16 Wyddial Lane."

"Himself? I thought he was going to send child protection people?"

"I don't know. He said he went himself."

"Do you think that means he passed it on to child protection and they weren't convinced enough to do anything?"

"I've no way of knowing."

"Try letting Dad speak," Zannah suggests.

"He talked to Kevin Cater and Yanina, and also to the children: Thomas and Emily. Had a nice long chat with them all, he said. In his opinion, all's well and there's nothing to worry about."

"Nothing to worry about?" *Don't lose it, Beth. Don't scream.*

Think about how insane Miss Hosmer sounded on Zannah's video. You don't want to sound like that. "What did you say, when he said that?" I ask.

"I thanked him for looking into it and for letting me know he had."

"That's all?"

"Yes. Should I have said something else? He'd done all he was going to do, and, let's face it, he needn't have done anything."

"But, Dad, you know there's something to worry about: all the things that still don't make sense."

"Pollard knows about those things too," I say quietly.

Dom looks past me into the middle distance, as if listening intently to someone behind me that I can't see or hear. I've got a strong feeling that person is begging him not to lose his temper.

"You're right, Beth. Pollard knows everything that's happened, he's been to the house, and the net result of all that is what I've just told you: he's satisfied nothing more needs to be done."

"And so we should be too? Did he go to Thomas's school? Did he talk to Lou Munday?"

"I don't know. He didn't say anything about the school."

"Course he didn't go to the school," says Zannah.

"Did he find out if Georgina Braid is dead or still alive?"

Dom looks puzzled—as if this is the last question he'd have expected me to ask. "He didn't mention Georgina at all."

"And you didn't either?"

"No, I didn't."

"Did he speak to any of the Caters' neighbors? Did you tell him about the shoes?"

"The . . ." He looks puzzled. Then he remembers. "No, I didn't tell him about Thomas Cater's fucking shoes!" Dom snaps. "I'm sick of this, Beth. Do you want to know why I didn't ask all the questions you wish I'd asked? I don't care anymore!

Whatever the Braids are up to, I don't give a shit, as long as I can get my life back—the life that didn't involve talking about the Braids and the Caters every waking second of every day."

"That's understandable," I say. Now that he's lost his temper, I feel calmer. "I've been expecting you to share my level of obsession. It wasn't fair of me. I'm sorry, okay?"

Dom eyes me suspiciously.

"I promise I'll stop talking to you about this soon," I say, knowing he won't notice the "to you," or think about what it might mean. "I have one more question: did Pollard say anything else, apart from what you've told me? Anything at all."

"Yes." Dom looks trapped. I know how he feels. I also know I'm not prepared to feel it for much longer. "He told me Kevin Cater admitted lying to us about his children's names. Cater told him he'd been reluctant to reveal the real names because he was worried you had a strange obsession with his children."

"Did he or Yanina admit that they both pretended she was Jeanette when we went around?"

"I don't know. That wasn't mentioned. And that was a second question. You said only one. I mean it, Beth. You can let this take over your life if you want, but I'm not letting it take over mine. If you want Pollard to do something else . . ."

"I don't want him to do anything."

"He spooned it." Zannah's voice rings with contempt.

"I'm the one who needs to find out what's going on," I say, thinking about Pam Swain's podcast exercise: *you imagine that each choice goes amazingly well, and then you choose which of those ideal outcomes would be the most ideal*. It doesn't work at all. My choice number two was leaving it up to Pollard to do what needs to be done. That's the one I chose, in my head, and look how it's turned out.

Or maybe Pam's exercise works brilliantly . . .

Yes. It does. You can't choose between two alternatives without thinking realistically about the people involved.

With Pollard being who he is, with his level of interest and care, and doing things in the way that he does them as a result, choice number two has already gone as well as it could have. For it to go any better, you'd need to replace Pollard with someone more determined, more obsessed, more willing to do whatever it takes—ideally, someone who once loved Flora Braid and her children.

I'd need to replace him with me. Which means choice number one is the right answer. "I have to do it myself," I tell Dom. "I'm the only person who can or ever would."

"What does that mean?" he asks. "Please don't say what I think you're about to say."

"It means going to Florida."

18

From: beth.leeson@triggerpointtherapy.co.uk
To: DominicL@Logonomika.com

Hi Dom,

I'm at Heathrow. My plane's delayed by two hours—great!

I don't think it's ever happened before that I've left the house with you refusing to speak to me or say good-bye. For what it's worth, I don't think it's fair. We've never disagreed about anything serious before, not once in our whole marriage. About this one thing we disagree, and that ought to be fine. Married couples don't always have to agree about everything.

You think a trip to Florida is an unnecessary expense. I don't. I need to do this. I think Flora and her kids might be in real trouble, and I can't just ignore that fear. No, she's not my friend anymore, but if I hadn't been so blinkered and pig-headed twelve years ago, maybe she still would be. I have to do what I can, and either I'll be able to help or I won't. Or I'll find my help isn't needed and I've been wrong about everything. Either way, I'll be glad I tried. And if I'm creating drama where there's no need, if I find out that I've been totally wrong to make a fuss, then I'll be relieved—and it will have been worth the money to find that out, because you're not the only one who wants their life back. I do too.

I wouldn't force you to go to Florida and spend more time on this, knowing you didn't want to. That wouldn't be fair. Can't you see that you trying to stop me when I feel I need to go is unfair too? I don't think it's irresponsible of me to go. I think it's the opposite.

All right, I'm going to stop now because I sound like a two-year-old: "It's not fair!" I'll be back as soon as I can, and the kids will be fine. Work will be fine. I sent a nice email to all my regulars and they all got back to me saying they understand completely, even though I hardly told them anything. I don't think I'm going to lose a single client. Zannah says she'll help around the house while I'm gone, and Ben won't worry as long as you don't panic him by making him think I've done something crazy. Instead, you could tell him that you support my decision to go to America, or at least that you understand it.

I'll ring you when I get to my hotel if it isn't too late.

B xxx

From: DominicL@Logonomika.com
To: beth.leeson@triggerpointtherapy.co.uk

I'm glad you emailed. Sorry I was off with you when you left. I'm just worried. But, yeah, I could have expressed it better. At the risk of sounding like a selfish twat, your safety is all I care about, not Flora's, and I don't like the idea of you walking up to Lewis Braid and calling him a liar to his face. The guy's not right in the head. He never was. We just didn't care because we were young and undiscriminating, and he threw great parties and was fun to hang around with (except when he wasn't). But I've been thinking—imagine being Flora all these years, having to live with him and deal with his bad side as well as his good side. He was always dead set on getting his way, and that tendency'll only have gotten worse as he's aged. For me, that explains why Flora's stressed and miserable, and why she ran away from you. If she feels trapped, if their relationship has turned ugly and she's too scared to leave him, she might not want you to see that. Neither of them would want you to see it.

Maybe I'm being over the top. I heard something on the radio this morning about coercive control in relationships. Some of the behaviors that were discussed sounded a bit like Lewis even as he was before, even without the getting-worse-with-age factor. That might have influenced me. Just don't meet him alone in any secluded places, okay? He might make a pass for all you know, and not take no for an answer.

This memory has just come back to me, a second ago: Lewis and I were having a drink at The Baron of Beef once and I said, "I wouldn't put anything past you, Braid" (I can't remember what made me say it) and he said, "You'd be right not to, Rom-com Dom." I still don't think he'd harm any children, though. That'd be a step too far even for him. But you're right: we can disagree about that. I just want to know that you're fine. Stay safe and come home soon.

D x

19

It's a little after eight in the evening, Florida time, when I arrive at the Delray Beach Marriott Hotel. According to my stiff body and aching brain, it's past one in the morning. The check-in desk, less than a minute's walk from the entrance doors, looks unfeasibly far away. Instead of feeling as if I've arrived, I'm looking at the reception staff and thinking, "Right, last leg of the journey, one final push." The prospect of having to fish out my passport and credit card, sign forms and make small talk makes me want to lie down on the floor and close my eyes.

The high-ceilinged lobby smells of several things all at once: mainly the sea, grilled meat, leather and suntan lotion. There's a heap of suitcases on the floor that looks as if it might once have been a pile. Children hop around them, try to sit on them, end up pushing them over. Grown-ups scoop their offspring up off the tiled floor and try to shush them. One little boy breaks free of his mother, runs over to a potted tree by the side of the entrance door and sticks his hands into the soil it's planted in.

Eventually, the suitcases and families are all processed and I'm at the front of the line for the reception desk. I hand over what I'm asked for and sign where I'm told to. Eventually, I get to my room, which contains two double beds. I lie down on one of them, stretch out and think about what I need to do before I can go to sleep: ring Dom, eat something . . .

Then I'm opening my eyes, feeling groggy. My throat is dry

and my bladder is uncomfortably full. What time is it? How long have I been asleep?

It takes me longer than it should to find my bag where I dropped it, on the far side of the other double bed, and pull out my phone.

It's 4 a.m., local time. My phone changed time zones in the taxi from the airport to the hotel, when I checked Lewis, Thomas and Emily Braid's social media accounts. None of them had posted anything new since I last looked.

Four a.m. That means I've been asleep for seven hours straight: conked out in my clothes, without brushing my teeth. And now I can't get into bed properly and sleep because I've done my night already and done it wrong.

I go to the bathroom and turn on the light. Good: there's a bathtub as well as a shower. And a little bottle of bubble bath lined up alongside the shampoo and conditioner. A long, hot, scented bath should be all I need to make me feel better. And food. Breakfast probably doesn't start till 6 a.m., but I can't wait till then. I'm starving.

What time will Lewis Braid get to his office? Seven thirty?

Or not at all, maybe. He might be on his way to the airport to fly to Japan on business, and you'll have wasted your time and money.

My stomach lurches at the thought. Then I realize it's not necessarily true. I might be able to find out more with Lewis gone than with him here in Florida. He won't have warned his colleagues not to tell me anything because it wouldn't occur to him that I'd turn up. If he's away on a business trip, I might be able to get his home address from someone if I play it right. I could go to the house, and if Flora's still here, which she might well be if Lewis wants to keep her well away from me . . .

Don't get carried away. Flora might not have been in America when she rang you. Lewis could have rigged it so that it looked as if that was where they were calling from.

They might both be in England.

Then where are seventeen-year-old Thomas and fifteen-year-old Emily? Home alone?

I need to think of a way to make Lewis's colleagues give me his home address. I searched online in the hope of finding a home address but nothing came up, so my obvious first port of call is Lewis's workplace, which was easy to find.

I chose this hotel because the offices of VersaNova are only a seven-minute drive away. *So close.* I try not to let myself believe this means I'm close to getting the answers I want. The more I hope this is nearly over, the more disappointed I'll be if my trip achieves nothing.

I dial the number for room service and skim-read the menu while I wait for someone to answer. Breakfast doesn't start till five thirty, so I order a pepperoni pizza from the all-night menu, telling myself that Italians must do it all the time. Then I brush my teeth, run my hands through my hair and wash my face, so that the waiter I'm about to meet won't mistake me for a scarecrow. The food, when it arrives, is delicious. I sit at the long black desk beneath the large TV screen on the wall, enjoying my early, inappropriate breakfast, and knowing I'd enjoy it more if I didn't think I might soon be face-to-face with Lewis Braid.

I've witnessed Lewis's anger a few times. Once in a restaurant, he yelled at a group of women at the next table who were making too much noise, and made such a forceful impression on them that they paid up and left before their main courses had been served—but I've never seen him angry with me. Not yet. How will he react when I turn up at his office, uninvited? Will he morph into a monster the way Camilla Hosmer did in Zannah's low-budget film?

Or maybe he's a monster already. It's so easy to believe that the label only fits infamous historical figures and mug-shot faces we see on the news. When it's someone in our personal life—someone we've sat laughing with in a pub, someone who's punted us down the River Cam singing "Sit Down, You're Rockin' the Boat" in a cheesy American accent—it's hard to believe that their true nature might be monstrous.

I think again about the incident in the restaurant. It happened while we were all still students. Flora and Lewis had only been an item for a few months. Two of the women from the noisy group were crying as they left the restaurant. I can't remember precisely what Lewis yelled at them, but it wasn't only about the racket they were making; it was more personal than that. He insulted their appearances and their intelligence—wittily and with his usual articulate brio, since every occasion and opportunity had to be The Lewis Braid Show. He wanted to solve the noise problem, but not as much as he wanted to make everyone else in the restaurant laugh.

None of us did. We looked down at the floor and wished it would swallow us up. I remember feeling ashamed to be out for dinner with someone who could behave in that way. Flora turned bright red and mumbled, "Lew-*is*," as she always did. He never normally had trouble raising a laugh, but he misjudged his audience on this occasion and took it too far.

Assuming I find him today, I'm going to need to talk to him alone in order to get anywhere.

I wonder if he'll deem it worth staging The Lewis Braid Show for me alone. Probably. One person is still an audience, though a small one. I expect his first move will be an attempt to lavish hospitality on me. *"Beth! What a fantastic surprise! It's so great to see you. Let me take you on a boat trip/to the best beach for miles around/to a baseball game!"*

When he realizes that I'm as determined to know the truth

as he is to keep it from me, will the friendly façade slip? And the question that really interests me: if it does, what will I see?

By 8 a.m., I'm already so tired that I could sleep for another seven hours if I let my eyes close. No chance of that. Not with Lewis Braid maybe about to arrive at any moment.

I'm sitting in the back of a taxi in the vast outdoor car park that belongs to his company, VersaNova. My driver called it a "parking lot." It's so well landscaped and generously proportioned, it almost seems to be the main point of this whole exercise—as if someone designed an enormous, attractive car park first, for its own sake, and then said, "You know what? It's a shame to waste this—let's put the head office of a multi-million-dollar tech company next to it."

Despite the early hour, I'm not the only person here. There are plenty of other cars around. None, yet, looks expensive enough to belong to Lewis Braid.

Now that I'm here at his workplace, in the full light of a day that promises to be warm and sunny, the thoughts I was thinking in my hotel room a few hours ago seem almost deranged. I came pretty close to wondering if Lewis was evil. He and Flora might be mixed up in something strange and unsavory—I'm certain they are, in fact—but there's a lot of distance between unsavory and monstrous. Lewis Braid is hardly a murderous villain.

You can handle him. You can handle the encounter you're about to have.

Assuming he comes into the office today.

I stare at the tanned, tire-shaped bulges of skin at the base of my taxi driver's skull and wish I could feel as calm as he seems. He's been luxuriating in silence all the way from the Marriott to VersaNova, as if wanting me to notice that it's a deliberate lifestyle choice. When I asked if he'd be happy to wait for as long as I need him to this morning, he did some slow, relaxed nodding. He has the manner of someone who would only emit words if you pierced a thick plastic seal inside him, turned him upside down and squeezed him hard.

I sit up straight as a car that looks like a contender pulls into the lot. It's low, flat, waxed to a powerful shine. No roof. *It's him. Lewis.*

I open the taxi's passenger door. "I'll be as quick as I can," I say to my driver as if he's urged me to hurry. His eyes are half closed. I'm not sure he's fully awake.

Lewis is quicker at getting out of cars than I am. By the time I'm out, he's several feet ahead, swinging a large black leather bag around and humming a tune—a gratingly fast-paced, bouncy one, if you're jet-lagged. Whatever he's hiding, he doesn't seem unduly worried about it.

He hasn't seen me. He's marching along briskly. Soon he'll reach the building, go inside, and then I'll have to deal with doormen, receptionists and probably security checks in order to get to him. He'll have a choice about whether to see me or not, whereas if I can get his attention now . . .

I open my mouth to yell his name, then notice that he's stopped suddenly, on the steps up to the revolving entrance door. He pulls a phone out of his pocket. Slowly, I move closer. He's facing the building, and has no idea that I'm approaching.

If he turns around and sees me, I'll say, "Hi, Lewis," as if I wanted him to notice me. Which I did, until this phone call happened. Now I'm hoping I can get close enough to listen, unobserved. The change in his body language tells me it isn't a run-of-the-mill conversation that he's having. He looks braced, somehow—as if the outcome of the call matters to him a lot. Maybe this is what all high-powered business calls look like.

I creep as close to him as I dare, then duck in between two

cars and kneel down so that I won't be visible if he decides he'd like a change of view while making his call. I hear him say, "Are you ready for Daily Responses? What?" he snaps. It sounds as if he's been told something he wasn't expecting to hear and doesn't like it much. "Ten minutes late, yes. Where are you?" he barks at whoever he's speaking to. "And where should you be?" he asks in the exact same tone after a short pause.

From cheery, haven't-a-care-in-the-world tune hummer to ice-cold Condemnatron boss in a few seconds. This is familiar; Lewis's demeanor used to change with dazzling speed when I knew him. In a minute he might be humming merrily again.

I hope so. That'll make it easier for me to pop up as soon as this phone call is over with my carefully rehearsed, "Hey, Lewis. You said I should come and visit you in Florida, so here I am!"

"And *what* are you?" he asks whoever he's speaking to.

Is he hoping for a response along the lines of "I'm a complete and utter fool whose entire life is a comprehensive failure"? It sounds like it. I wouldn't be surprised if someone's out of a job before the day is over.

"Good," says Lewis, sounding placated. Evidently his interlocutor has said the right thing. "I'll see you later."

Maybe the correct answer to "*What* are you?" and the one supplied, was "On my way in right now to apologize profusely and beg your forgiveness."

I wonder what Daily Responses is. Is Lewis on his way there now? It sounds like a strange kind of religious service—like the masses I used to attend at my Catholic school. They involved prayers and responses. VersaNova must have a daily ritual that's the secular equivalent. This being America, it probably involves yoga, green tea and affirmations.

If Lewis's colleague is ten minutes late, doesn't that mean he is too? Maybe the colleague is supposed to be there already, before him.

He puts his phone back in his pocket, turning slightly. I duck down lower. Having him see me is one thing; being caught eavesdropping is another.

That could happen. He could, at this moment, be striding toward my hiding place.

All I can do is wait, crouch and pray. Time passes. No one appears. Once I think it's safe, I stand up and rub the small of my back.

The steps are empty. There's no sign of Lewis anywhere in the car park. He must have gone inside.

Damn.

Though it's not necessarily a bad thing. Talking inside beats talking in a car park, assuming he agrees to see me. And if he refuses, I'll know for certain that I'm on the right track. A Lewis Braid with no guilty conscience would come bounding out of his office to greet an old friend.

VersaNova's lobby is covered, bottom to top, in glossy veined stone of an indeterminate noncolor. At its center is a reception desk made of the same stone that looks as if it has grown up out of the floor. Three receptionists are lined up behind the desk, looking like hopeful contestants in a game show with a ludicrously high budget. Above their heads, there's a large silver plaque embedded in the wall, bearing VersaNova Techologies' logo.

Two of the receptionists are smiling too hard at me. I walk over to the third. She looks the least suspiciously radiant. "I'd like to speak to Lewis Braid," I tell her. "I just saw him arrive." On her name badge it says "Wayna Skinner" and, beneath that, "I make sure to want from a feeling of abundance."

As I suspected: yoga, green tea and affirmations.

I can't see the badge of the receptionist on the far left—it's too far away—but the one in the middle, Lisa Pearce, has some words of wisdom on her badge too: "Failure only lasts forever if I'm too scared to try again." I might suggest they introduce similar badges at Bankside Park: "Camilla Hosmer. Lies, false accusations and sporadic racism keep me looking young."

I think about what Lewis said on the phone about having a favorite life coach. Was it his idea to pin inspiring messages to the company's receptionists? It wouldn't surprise me, though the Lewis I knew had no time at all for new-age nonsense. America might have changed him, I suppose, or he might be cynically playing the corporate game. I wonder if he'll be willing to miss Daily Responses in order to talk to me.

"Do you have an appointment with Dr. Braid?" Wayna Skinner asks me.

"No."

"Then you'll need to make one. He doesn't see anyone without an appointment."

"Can you tell him Beth Leeson is here? I think he'll see me. Tell him I've come all the way from England, in response to his invitation the other night. I'm an old friend."

"Oh, I see. Awesome. Let me see what I can do for you." She picks up the phone. "Martha? It's Wayna. There's a lady here to see Dr. Braid. A Beth Leeson. She's an old friend he invited over. Thank you."

I wish I could witness the moment of Martha telling Lewis I'm here: downstairs, in his building. What will he think? How will he react?

"I sure will. Thank you, Martha." Wayna hangs up the phone. "He'll see you. Please stand in front of the camera and I'll take a photo for your pass."

"Camera?"

"Up there. Can I see your ID? Passport?"

Luckily I still have it in my bag, from the airport. I trust my own ability to look after my handbag more than I trust any hotel safe.

With her friendly smile fixed in place, Wayna stares at my passport photograph and me for longer than anyone in an airport ever has. "My hair was different then," I tell her.

Finally she places a laminated pass in my hands with excessive care, as if she's granting me access to the country's nuclear codes. The photograph VersaNova's camera has taken of me from on high makes my head look huge and my body tiny and tapering.

"Take the elevator up to five and Martha will meet you there," she says. "Have a great visit!"

The elevator is good company. It lets rip with an exuberant, prerecorded "Level! Five!" as we come to a stop. The doors open and I step out into a beige-carpeted reception area. There are two sets of white double doors and four orange leather chairs lined up against one wall, but no Martha. I'm wondering if I ought to do anything apart from wait when one of the doors swings open.

"Lewis."

"Beth! It's really you! Is Dom with you?"

"No. Just me."

"You should have brought the whole family. What a treat it is to see you!" He strides over and wraps me in a hug. I think about resisting, even as I hug him back. In his best moments, this was what was great about spending time with Lewis. He could make you feel as if you were his favorite treat in a way that no one else could.

"Maybe some other time," I say. "I came alone because . . . I'm not on holiday. This isn't a fun trip for me."

"Isn't it?" Lewis laughs. "So you're here to work? Great! Our latest prototype needs to be ready for market in five months. Want to help with that?"

"I want some answers. Ones that are true." I try to say this hopefully, as if I believe he's going to help me.

"Well, you've come to the right place. I'm always happy to

give true answers to true questions. But let's hold this Q and A in my office, where we can have some privacy—in case this turns out to be like the drinking games we used to play. Remember those? Share a sordid secret or down one more shot."

Something about his manner makes me wonder if he's prepared for this. Did he expect that one day I'd come here and appeal directly to him? Did he take steps to make sure I soon ran out of other options, relishing the prospect of using his charm to turn Beth-the-problem into Beth-who's-no-threat-at-all?

I laugh and try to look impressed and amused, knowing that's what he wants. I need to choose my words carefully—to make this The Beth Leeson Show, directed by me and not Lewis, unlike every other interaction I've ever had with him.

"I haven't brought any alcohol with me, but we could maybe play a variant of that game," I say as I follow him along a gleaming white corridor.

"Without the best bit? How would that work? Would there be any refreshments at all? I've got the wherewithal to make us some beautiful mint tea in my office."

"Great. So the new game can be sordid-secret swapping," I say smoothly. "We can drink mint tea and swap secrets." It's not as hard to talk like this as it would be to anyone who wasn't Lewis. I'd forgotten this about him: in order for a conversation with him to work, you often had to imitate his manner, and you hoped no one heard you doing it.

"I refuse to believe you have any sordid secrets, Beth." We've stopped. He opens a door and gestures for me to go in.

"Maybe not sordid, but I do have secrets," I say, staying where I am, in the corridor. "Doesn't everybody?"

"I don't think so. Imagine that." Lewis looks serious suddenly. "Imagine having none at all. Wouldn't that be horrible?"

"I'm not sure."

"Nothing that you'd mind everyone knowing about you,

nothing that you keep just for you and maybe a few trusted friends? I'd hate it."

Don't ask him to tell you his secret. Not yet. It's too soon.

"Am I your trusted friend?" I say instead.

A grin spreads across his face. "I could slip easily into people-pleasing mode and say yes, but you said you wanted true answers, so. I don't know, Beth. You and Dom disappeared from my life in kind of a weird way. What was that all about? Flora would never tell me. She wanted me to believe we'd all drifted apart but I don't think that's what happened, is it?"

"No."

"No. I told Flora I didn't believe that story, so she made up a better one, hoping I'd like it more: some nonsense about you cutting up a photo of our children."

"That's true. I did. But I don't think that's why our friendship ended."

"It's *true*?" Lewis laughs. He looks delighted—as if it's the best news he's heard in a long time. He reaches out and squeezes my shoulder. The doors at the far end of the corridor open and two women appear. Lewis waves in their direction without really looking at them, then gestures again through his open office door. "Come on in," he says. "I haven't got long, but I want you all to myself for the time we do have. Something tells me you and I are going to have *fun* today."

20

There's a framed photograph on Lewis's desk: of him, Thomas and Emily sitting outside a beachfront restaurant, under a green-and-white-striped awning. All three of them have lobsters in front of them and they're all laughing.

"No Flora?" I say, pointing to it. "No Georgina?"

"In that particular photo?" says Lewis. He moves over to inspect it more closely. "I've never seen either of them, and I work next to that photo most days of my life. But let me know if you spot something I've missed. Mint tea? Once I've made it, I'll take the photo out of its frame and you can cut it up if you like. It's okay, I've got plenty more." He grins to make it clear he's joking.

"You didn't want a reminder of all four of them on your desk?"

"I'm fascinated by these questions." Lewis arranges white square mugs in square saucers at the drinks station beneath his huge, metal-framed window. "I change the picture all the time," he says. He sounds gleeful. If he wishes I hadn't turned up in his new American life, he's doing an excellent job of concealing it. "This week it's Thomas and Emily's turn in the frame. Everyone gets a turn. Just like, at home, I change my colleague picture regularly. On the mantelpiece in the living room, I currently have a framed photo of Aaron and David from Marketing."

I laugh. I think it's convincing.

"So, when does the secret-swapping start?" Lewis asks, handing me my tea.

"Soon as you like. I'll go first. I cut up a family photo Flora sent me—one that came with a Christmas card. Actually, I didn't cut it up completely. I just cut Georgina out of it."

I watch Lewis's face to see if anything changes when I mention her name. It doesn't. All I see is intense curiosity and relish, no discomfort or guilt. No sadness either.

"Go on," says Lewis. "I'm intrigued."

"I'd have thought you'd be disgusted, or furious," I say. "Georgina was only a tiny baby. I cut her out of a photograph of your family. She fell on the floor."

"So what?" Lewis chuckles. "This was more than ten years ago. Whatever you did, you did it to a piece of paper, not to my daughter. I'd love to know why, though." He walks over to his desk, sits behind it, then uses it as a footstool, putting his feet up on a pile of glossy brochures.

I try to focus on his face, not the soles of his shoes. "When I saw the picture, I realized Flora had been pregnant and had a baby, and not told me. I took that as evidence of how little I mattered to her. The photo she sent was the first I knew of Georgina's existence. I was upset, and I overreacted. Then I felt terrible about it. Flora found out I'd done it, which didn't help our friendship, but that wasn't the cause of the rift between us. That was something else."

"Was it a rift? Is that what it was?" asks Lewis. "A rift sounds dramatic and exciting. You're telling me a rift happened and I missed it? I'll be honest: I always thought the root cause was envy."

"Because you suddenly had money? No. For a long time I thought it was the money that had changed things between us, but I was wrong."

"Then what was it?"

"That's what I'm waiting for you to tell me."

"Well . . . let's see." He smiles conspiratorially, as if we're both enjoying the game. "I've never cut up any photographs of your children."

"You know what I want you to tell me, Lewis."

His face changes. The smile is gone. Now he's staring at me earnestly, with sympathy in his eyes. "I think I do," he says. "I think you want a story that explains why you've seen Flora in England recently. The thing is, Beth, you can't have. Flora hasn't been in England. She's been here, with her family. I don't know who you saw, but it wasn't her."

"Maybe I saw the woman who lives there now," I say.

"Quite possibly."

"Jeanette Cater?"

"I can't remember her name, if it's even the same family that we sold to."

"Don't you remember Kevin and Jeanette Cater?"

"Kevin Cater . . . Yes, I think that is who we sold to."

"You used to work with him."

"No, I didn't."

"He worked at CEMA while you and Flora were there."

"Did he?" Lewis looks mildly interested in this coincidence. "You could be right, but I didn't know him. Flora might have. Beth, are you all right? You're starting to worry me."

"I'm fine. Do you have a current photo of Georgina? I'd like to see one."

"Not with me, no."

"None on your phone?"

"No."

"How come?"

"Do you know about Georgina?" Lewis asks. "I suppose you might have found out if you've been scouring the UK in search of Flora."

"What's there to know?"

"That she died," Lewis says simply. "Which . . . you knew. Okay. Did Flora's parents tell you?"

"Why did you lie to me? I asked you how old she was now and you said twelve."

"I didn't want to discuss the death of my daughter with someone who's not part of my life anymore. My aim was to get on to a new subject as swiftly as possible. I miscalculated, clearly, because now we're having the conversation I didn't want to have, only face-to-face."

No. He sounds so plausible, but it can't be true. Or rather, what he's told me so far might be true but he's saying it to obscure the bigger truth, whatever that is. If he really had nothing to hide, why would he allow someone he hasn't spoken to for twelve years to intrude into his morning with a barrage of strange questions? He wouldn't. He'd ask me to leave.

"I'm sorry Georgina died," I say.

"Thank you. Me too." Lewis smiles sadly. "This game turned out to be less fun than I hoped it would be."

"Tell me the truth, Lewis. Please."

"I just have."

"The whole truth." I'm not scared to push him further. What's he going to do, leap out of his chair and punch me? I'm assuming he cares what the people in this building think of him and so wouldn't risk it. "If you and Flora are still married, why are there no photos of her on your Instagram? Why is she living with Kevin Cater in your old house, and calling herself Jeanette? Whose are the two children that live in that house? They're yours and Flora's, aren't they? So why are they living with Kevin Cater? I've *seen* them, Lewis. I know you're their father."

"Are you lonely, Beth?"

"No. I'm not lonely at all."

"Are you fulfilled?"

"What do you mean?"

"You've flown all the way from England to sit in my office and fire strange accusations at me. They do sound like accusations, whether that's your intention or not—as if you're a TV detective trying to crack a case. Which casts me in the role of 'villain you've exposed, about to be locked up at Her Majesty's pleasure.' In fact, I'm someone who's done nothing wrong and who used to be your friend. Whose third child died tragically many years ago, and who didn't and doesn't want to talk about that with someone he's no longer close to. There's nothing in my life that justifies a manic interrogation, so . . . this has to be about whatever's going on with you. I'm wondering if you're okay."

I decide to try a new tactic. "Tell me the truth, Lewis. I don't much care what it is. All I want is to know. People are trying to tell me I didn't see something I know I saw, and I've had enough. At least confirm that it was Flora I saw, even if you won't tell me anything else."

A flicker of impatience passes across his face. "Beth, I can take you to Flora right now if you like."

"She might be in Florida now, but she wasn't the two times I saw her."

"Yes, she was." Lewis raises one hand, finger pointed upward. "I've thought of a solution.

"Can you tell me the exact dates and times of your alleged Flora sightings? There's rarely a day that she doesn't see someone—her friends, charity committee ladies, tennis club people. I can probably track down whoever she was with when you claim to have seen her in the UK."

"To provide an alibi, you mean?" An extremely well-paid one, no doubt. "I'm sure you could, but why would you? If you're telling the truth and nothing suspicious is going on, why would you indulge my irrational obsession?"

"The very question I'm asking myself at the moment." Lewis smiles again. "Because you were once a good friend, I guess. As for something suspicious . . . even if Flora was in the UK, which she wasn't, how is that suspicious? She has a passport. She's allowed to travel."

"The two children living at 16 Wyddial Lane are called Thomas and Emily."

Lewis laughs. "Yeah, right. Of course they are."

"I heard Flora call them by those names. They look identical to . . ." I point at the photo on his desk. "To the way *they* looked at the same age. That's how I know they're yours."

"Wait, wait . . ." For the first time since I arrived, he looks as if he doesn't know exactly what to say next. "Beth, I don't want to hurt your feelings, but . . . do you realize how unwell you sound?"

"I might sound that way to someone else, who knew nothing, but it's not how I sound to you. To you, I sound like someone who knows a bit too much. Whereas to me, I sound like someone who knows too little."

"This is verging on pathological now," he says.

"We could easily sort it out once and for all."

"How?"

"Take me to see Thomas and Emily. If they tell me Flora lives with you all and hasn't been in England recently, I might believe them."

"You know what?" He sounds angry. Finally. "I'm not going to do that. I'm not going to introduce my kids to someone displaying pathologically obsessive behavior. Even if she is an old friend."

"All right. Never mind. They'd probably lie for you anyway if you paid them enough. If mine are anything to go by, teenagers are generally bribe-able."

"Are you listening to yourself? Can you hear how you sound?"

"Who's Chimpy?"

"Chimpy?" I see a flash of what looks like genuine confusion. "I have no idea who Chimpy is. Who is it?"

"I don't know. I think you do, though." As I say it, I'm aware that it doesn't feel true.

He doesn't know. Everything else I've said, even if he wasn't expecting it, he knew it might come up. But not this. Not Chimpy.

"What's happened to you, Beth? Hearing you say these things . . . it makes me ashamed for you. How have you become this? I can withstand any attack you want to launch at me, but it makes me sad for you."

"Nothing you say is going to work on me," I tell him. "Not until you tell me the truth."

"All right, well . . ." He shrugs. "I guess we're done here."

"Are we? You're not curious about anything I've said? If you don't believe the two children living in your old house are called Thomas and Emily, you could easily check. Ring Huntingdon police and ask for PC Paul Pollard. He'll tell you."

"The police? You went to the police about this?"

I nod. "I'm worried about the children. And Flora. She would never have cut off her parents and stopped them from seeing their grandchildren. Not of her own free will."

"Ah, I see. You think I'm controlling Flora? Stopping her making her own decisions?"

"She was always scared of you. I didn't see it at the time, but now I see it as clearly as I see you standing here in front of me. All those times she mumbled, 'Lew-*is*,' when you were off on one of your rants. I always assumed she was embarrassed, but she wasn't. She was scared. That was her way of begging you to stop—and even that she could only bring herself to do in the mildest way. That's why I didn't recognize it for the fear it was. And I think it must have gotten worse and worse. The last time you all came around was the worst I've ever seen it. Do you remember ordering Flora out of our living room so that we wouldn't catch a glimpse of her breasts while she fed Georgina? She obeyed without question. She always obeyed you, but on that day she looked properly scared. I was too wrapped up in my own guilt about that stupid photo to notice at the time, but I remember it vividly. That was fear I saw on her face. Fear of you."

"I feel this is where I should say, 'Much as I'd like to spend the morning talking about my wife's breasts . . .'" Neither of us laughs. Lewis says, "You're scraping the barrel, Beth. Her *breasts*? I don't know what you're talking about. I don't remember . . . No, I'll go even further. I don't think anything like that happened the last time we all got together. In fact, I'm sure it didn't. Flora sunbathes topless on beaches all over the world. You know she does: you've been on holiday with us enough times to know. People in every continent have seen her tits and I don't give a shit. Wow." He exhales slowly. "That's something I didn't expect to be saying this morning."

"You're not going to make me doubt myself, Lewis. I've spoken to Tilly from number 3 Wyddial Lane. The woman you stalked, remember?"

"You want to talk about stalking?" He's not quite shouting, but he's almost there.

I'm in the middle of the room. He's behind his desk. I could make a dash for the door and I'd get to it before he could stop me.

If I need to. I still don't think he'll turn violent. His losses of temper were always verbal only. I never saw him hit anything or anyone. He wouldn't risk me running out of the room yelling that Lewis Braid had assaulted me.

"What is it that you're doing if not stalking, Beth? Coming all the way to America to tell me about some children that are nothing to do with me . . . My life, Flora's life, it's none of your fucking business. I owe you nothing. No explanations, nothing! You have the nerve to say Flora's scared of me? You're the one she's scared of. Not me. *You.* She never runs away from *me.*"

My breath catches in my throat. Does he realize what he's done? Lewis closes his eyes. He slumps a little in his chair.

Yes. He realizes.

"So you admit Flora was in Huntingdon—that I saw her there, and that she ran away from me in the car park? There's no point in denying it now. We both heard what you just said."

I count the seconds, waiting for an answer. Finally, he gives a small nod.

Thank you. I wasn't wrong and I'm not crazy.

"Why would Flora be scared of me?"

"Because she needed you to leave her alone, and you wouldn't. Instead, you turned into a stalker."

"Needed me to leave her alone, or wanted me to?"

"I can't answer that," Lewis says wearily. "I'm not her."

"What do you mean?"

"You'll find out soon enough. Come on." He pushes back his chair and stands up. "I'm not having this conversation without Flora."

"Where are we going?"

"Do you want answers? I thought that's why you came here— for answers?"

"It is."

"Then you need to trust me, or you won't get any. Which might be better for everybody, but it's too late for that. You won't leave it alone, so you're going to get your answers—whatever the cost, right?"

"What do you mean?"

He looks as if he's weighing whether to say what's on his mind. "Since Georgina died, Flora hasn't been . . . She's not the same person you remember, as you've so observantly noticed. Seeing and speaking to you will make her much worse. *That's why we've been trying to keep you at bay.* It's not going to help Flora to share intimate details of our life to satisfy your curiosity. It's not going to help me either, as the person who has to look after Flora—which is why I'd very much appreciate it if you'd turn around, go home and forget all about us. But you're not going to do that, are you?"

How has he done it? How has he gone from lying brazenly to my face to making me feel guilty?

He's a liar. The guilt you're feeling is a lie. Don't let him see it.

"If you want to protect Flora from having to talk to me, you could easily do that," I tell him. "Give me an explanation that makes sense."

"It wouldn't be fair to do that without involving Flora. It's her story to tell as much as mine. Where are you staying? A hotel?"

"The Marriott, Delray Beach."

"Go there now. Flora and I will meet you there in an hour, hour and a half. Soon as we can."

Will you? Or will you take Flora and the kids and run?

I can't think of any way to stop him from leaving his office and going wherever he wants. I can hardly block his way to the door, or lock him in.

Locked up at Her Majesty's pleasure . . . Lewis said it before and it stuck in my mind.

Wait. What if . . .

An idea is starting to form in my mind. Of all the expressions Lewis might have used, he chose that one. *He* chose it: Lewis Braid.

I'll need to check to see if I could be right. A simple Internet search will sort that out.

"I'll see you at the Marriott," I say as evenly as I can manage.

"Are you all right?" Lewis asks. "You look a bit . . ."

"I'm fine."

"What room are you in at the hotel?"

"We won't be going to my room," I tell him. "I'll meet you in the lobby."

We leave the building together. Lewis smiles and waves at the three receptionists on his way out. I hand my laminated pass back to Wayna.

Once we're outside, Lewis heads for his car without looking at me or saying good-bye. I walk over to my taxi, more grateful to be reunited with my silent driver than I would have believed possible.

As we pull out of VersaNova's car park, I fumble in my bag for my phone. It won't take long to search for the name that I might have invented . . .

A few seconds later, I have the confirmation I need. And no idea at all what it might mean.

21

I'm sitting in the lobby of the Marriott, facing the main doors, when Lewis and Flora walk in. *At last.* It's nearly two hours since Lewis and I left VersaNova together. He looks preoccupied and determined, as if he's in the middle of completing an important task and nobody had better interrupt him until it's done. He's still holding his black leather bag, the same one he had with him at the office. Flora looks at me, then quickly looks away, as if she might still avoid an encounter with me if she plays this right.

It occurs to me only now, when I see them together: he looks a lot younger than she does. That never used to be true. Whatever they've been through, she's come out of it worse.

I stand up and walk toward them. Flora stops. For a moment, I wonder if she might turn and run again. Lewis drapes his arm over her shoulder. Anyone else in the hotel lobby who observed the gesture would think it was affectionate: a man putting his arm around his wife. To me it looks as if Lewis also fears Flora might try and escape.

None of us says hello. Lewis says, "Let's go to your room, Beth."

"I told you, I'm not doing that. We can sit there and talk." I point to an octagonal space nearby, marked out by eight white floor-to-ceiling pillars. Between the pillars, on a raised platform, there are tables and chairs. "No one's sitting there. We'd have it to ourselves."

"I'm not doing this in a public place," says Lewis. "Either we go to your room or Flora and I leave. What do you think we're going to do to you, Beth?"

My room has a balcony that overlooks the swimming-pool terrace, where there are bound to be a good number of people sunbathing or reading on loungers. If I leave the door to the balcony wide open, so that I can shout for help if I need to . . .

"Can I see what's inside your bags before you bring them into my room?" I say.

"From TV detective to airport security." Lewis shakes his head.

I don't care how disappointed he is in me. I don't trust him and I'm not taking any risks. I've never trusted anyone less, in fact. He needn't be here, with a story he's reluctant but prepared to tell me. There's only one reason why he'd bring Flora here and give up his working day to explain things to me that—as he correctly pointed out—are none of my business: he's still hoping to control me. He wants to satisfy my curiosity because he fears what will happen if he doesn't.

"You can look in Flora's bag." He pulls it off her shoulder and hands it to me. "Mine's full of confidential documents. I can leave it in the car, if it bothers you?"

"Yes, please."

"Fine. Give me five minutes." Flora tries to follow him when he moves to leave the lobby. "What are you doing?" he asks her.

"Coming with you."

"Why? Wait here."

He leaves. Flora stares down at the ground.

"Are you angry with me?" I ask her.

"No. Of course not."

"I wish you and I could talk alone."

"We can't," she says quickly.

"Now? Or ever?"

"We won't see each other again after today."

"Why? Because Lewis won't let you see me again?"

"We only agreed to meet you so that you'd leave us alone. You need to stop . . . what you're doing. Stop following me around." She looks up at me. There are tears in her eyes. "I don't want to see you."

"I'm not here because I want us to be friends again," I say. "If you don't want that then I don't either. All I want is to know that you and your children are all right—your two youngest children, who have the same names as your two oldest. Don't they?"

She says nothing. Her eyes flit back and forth.

"Why, Flora? Why would you do that? I've seen Yanina picking Thomas up. They didn't look at each other or speak to each other. I'm worried for him and Emily. I saw him walking along with the sole of his shoe hanging off. Even if you don't care about yourself, you should care about those children."

"I care," she says.

"Well, then, you must know they're not okay. And you're not okay either. Let me help. Tell me what's going on before Lewis comes back. We don't have to wait here for him. We could go somewhere else where—"

"I don't need your help. I don't need you to worry about me."

"If you don't want to talk to me, why are you here?"

"Lewis says we have to, otherwise you won't ever leave us alone, and that's all I want: for you to leave me alone." Instead, Lewis has left her alone with me. Why? He could have easily let her go with him to the car.

It would have looked odd, though—her trotting after him like a slave. And he knows he's trained her well enough that she won't say anything. Unless . . . No. Unless nothing. Every time I find myself starting to wonder if maybe Flora's the one in control, I think back to the way she and Lewis were when I knew them before.

He's the boss. Always was, always will be.

"Who's Chimpy?" I ask.

Flora looks puzzled, as I expected her to. "Chimpy? I don't know."

"I'm sorry about Georgina," I tell her. "When I saw you outside your house in Hemingford Abbots, you were talking on the phone. I heard you say that you were very lucky. To lose a child isn't lucky."

"You think I don't know that?"

"Why did you describe yourself as lucky? It might sound like a strange question, but I heard you say it twice. Once was outside the house and the other time was when Lewis first rang me, after I sent him a message on Instagram. I heard you in the background saying those exact same words: 'I'm very lucky.'"

"I *am* lucky." She looks away. "Only people with nothing to live for are unlucky. Do you think that because Georgina died, I have nothing to live for? I have other children, and I love them."

"How many?"

"What?"

"How many other children do you have? What are their names?"

"How can you do this to me?" she whispers. "I've told you I don't want it. The children are fine."

"Flora, they're not. They're . . ." *Too late.* Lewis is back. My time alone with Flora has run out. I try not to feel frustrated. It's not as if the conversation was going well.

"I'm good to go," Lewis says. "No bag, no concealed weapons." He twirls around. "Do you want to pat me down?"

"Wait here," I say. "I need to use the bathroom. Then we can go up."

"There's probably one in your room." He smiles. "I'll help you find it."

"I'm not leaving the two of you alone in my hotel room."

"Worried we'll snoop around in all your private stuff? I think that's what they call projection."

"Wait here. I won't be long."

Locked inside a cubicle, I repeat to myself the words, "You are not at risk of physical harm" until I believe them. Then I pull my phone out of my bag, go to Voice Memos and press the "Record" button. I don't know what story I'm about to be told or if any of it will be true, but I want it on record, whatever it turns out to be.

Up in my room, I decide I'm not going to open the door to the balcony. Now that we're all here, the feeling that I might be in danger has evaporated, and the only thing worrying me is that I'm about to waste more time listening to lies. How would I know?

Lewis and Flora sit in the two chairs opposite the desk and TV. I sit on the edge of the bed nearest them. "Well?" I say, putting my bag down on the floor in front of my feet. Hopefully it will be close enough for the recording to work.

"What do you want to know?" Lewis asks. "We'll answer your questions on two conditions. One: that you leave us alone afterward and don't reappear in our lives at any point in the future, for any reason. Can you give us that guarantee?"

"If you tell me the truth, and if the children aren't at risk of harm."

"The children are fine. Though I'm not sure which children you mean. Presumably the younger two?" Lewis raises a hand to silence me. "Between us, Flora and I have four children. All of them are safe, loved and well looked after."

"What's your other condition?" I ask him.

"Confidentiality. You can tell Dominic. I know him well enough to know he won't say anything. I assume he's still a fan of the path of least resistance?"

"He won't tell anybody."

"Good. Impress on him that he mustn't. And you tell no one apart from him. Understood?"

I nod. Lewis must be delusional if he thinks it's a real promise. I'll tell whoever the hell I feel like telling—whoever I think needs to know.

"Thank you," he says. "It's all yours, Beth. Ask away."

"Why did you lie? Why pretend you and Flora are still together? You're not still together, are you?"

"No."

"And Flora's married to Kevin Cater?"

"Yes. Though she's not called Flora anymore. Her legal name is Jeanette Cater."

I turn to Flora. "Why did you change it? And if you're married to Kevin Cater, why do you live in the same house you lived in with Lewis? Why call your children Thomas and Emily when you've already got two children with those names?"

"Flora?" Lewis prompts. "I'm not doing this on my own."

"And why are they *your* children, if she's with Kevin now?" I ask him. "They're not Kevin's. I've seen them. They're yours. They have your eyes, like the other Thomas and Emily. I thought they were the same people. I thought the Thomas and Emily I knew hadn't grown in twelve years—that's how similar they look."

"They're Kevin's children," says Flora. "Mine and Kevin's. You're right, they look like . . . their older half-brother and sister, and their eyes aren't Lewis's. There are brown-eyed people in my family. My mum has brown eyes like that. Maybe they're her eyes. I know I always said they were the spitting image of Lewis's but I never really believed it."

"She only said it to keep me happy," says Lewis. "They both had her face, and she thought I'd mind. I probably would have, in those days. I was still an emotional child when we had our kids."

"Why did you give the children you had with Kevin the same names?" I ask Flora.

"Georgina's death . . ." she starts to say.

"What? What about it?"

She seems to have frozen. We wait for nearly ten seconds. Then she turns to Lewis. "I can't," she says. "You."

She sounds like a small child. *You do it, Daddy.*

Lewis rubs his temples with the flats of his hands. "Me," he says in a low voice. "All right. You want my version? Flora's never heard my version before, not in my words. Why would she? She already knows the story, so I've never needed to tell her, but she seems to want to hear it now. She won't like it much, but okay. You sure you don't want to take over?" he asks her.

She shakes her head.

Lewis looks at me. "You won't like it either. Georgina didn't die of natural causes. Gerard and Rosemary no doubt told you it was Sudden Infant Death Syndrome. It wasn't. It was neither natural nor unavoidable. Georgina died because Flora made two bad decisions. One: to have Georgina sleep in our bed. Thomas never did, Emily didn't . . . but Georgina was premature and Flora was neurotic about her. For no reason that I could fathom, she wanted Georgina in bed next to her every night. Insisted it would be better for her. Fine—she was the mother, and I assumed she knew what she was talking about. I moved into the spare room. Couldn't sleep properly with a snuffling baby that close.

"One night, I came home to find Flora halfway down a bottle of white wine. I was surprised. She didn't normally drink, but she'd had a tough day with all three kids being difficult in some way. Still, I told her to take it easy. She said she was fine, she'd only had a couple of glasses. I told her that was more than enough and she swore at me—said it was none of my fucking business. It was the first time she'd ever spoken to me like that.

"We had a big row. I went up to my office—my office at home—slammed the door and worked for the rest of the evening. Flora gave the children their baths. That was supposed to be my job, but that night I didn't care. I was too angry. I heard Flora putting Thomas and Emily to bed, heard them asking why Daddy wasn't joining in. Then she must have taken Georgina and gone to bed because I didn't hear anything else. At about ten thirty, I realized I hadn't eaten and was starving. Flora hadn't brought me up any supper, which I took to mean that she was still angry with me. I looked in the fridge and the oven—nothing. So I went out. Drove into Huntingdon, got myself a curry. Came home, went to bed in the spare room. I was still pretty angry, and wondering what I'd do if Flora didn't apologize first thing in the morning. There was no way I was putting up with treatment like that. I went to sleep."

He seems to be steeling himself to continue. Finally he says, "A few hours later, I was woken by screaming from Flora. I ran to our bedroom and found Georgina lying there, dead. In our bed. She was blue. Not breathing. It was the worst moment of my life."

"I killed her," Flora says, her voice no more than a whisper. "I didn't murder her deliberately. What I did was worse, because I didn't want her to die but I still caused it to happen: the opposite of what I wanted. Even though I'd drunk that wine, I still put Georgina down by my side, as I always did. Normally it was fine."

"And this one night it wasn't," says Lewis. "Flora rolled on top of her and suffocated her."

"So now you know." Flora looks at me. "I'm a woman who got drunk and killed her baby."

"That's why you cut your parents out of your life," I say, starting to understand.

"Not just them," says Flora. "Everybody. Lewis, Thomas, Emily. You."

"What do you mean?"

"Lewis didn't want our marriage to end. Even after what I'd done. It was me. Lewis tried to help me. He was heroic. I didn't want help, though. I wanted to pretend it had never happened—and that meant getting far, far away from anyone who had known or cared about Georgina. The other two children, and Lewis . . ." Flora shakes her head. "They were my victims as much as she was. I'd deprived them of a sister, a daughter. I'd deprived my parents of a grandchild. I had to get away from all of them."

"And me?"

"No!" She says it as if having me in her life would have been the worst torment of all. "We'd been so close, Beth. You'd have sensed I was hiding something and dragged the truth out of me. And even if you hadn't, don't you understand? I couldn't tolerate any continuity with my old life. The only way I could live at all was in a world that had never known Georgina. If I could have erased everyone's memory . . . Obviously I couldn't, but I made Lewis vow never to tell the others what had happened."

"By the others, do you mean Thomas and Emily?" I ask.

Flora nods.

Lewis says, "It was bad enough that they'd lost their baby sister. Neither Flora nor I could stand the thought of them knowing the full truth: that their own mother's negligence had killed her. And no one else could know the truth either, least of all the authorities. Flora might have gone to prison for all we knew. Then Thomas and Emily would have a mother behind bars, I'd have a wife who was a convict. No. Intolerable. Believe me, Beth, I was as keen to conceal the truth as Flora was."

A tear rolls down Lewis's cheek and he wipes it away. I've never seen him cry before. I don't like it; it feels wrong.

"It was much easier to say that we'd found Georgina dead and had no idea why she'd stopped breathing," he goes on. "Thomas and Emily were too young to connect that with the row they'd overheard the night before, me telling Flora to stop drinking."

"I couldn't go to prison," says Flora. "That would have been the thing . . ." She trails off.

"What?" I ask her.

"I was too scared to take my own life, after Georgina died. I wanted to, more than anything—to never feel anything ever again. Couldn't make myself go through with it. But if there was even a chance I'd go to prison I'd have done it."

"So you called it cot death and everyone believed you?"

"The parents don't get to call an infant death anything," says Lewis. "Doctors decide. We told everyone that we'd found Georgina in her cot, blue and not breathing. People couldn't have been more sympathetic. There was no hint of any suspicions in our direction. But Georgina had been born premature, and was maybe going to need surgery on her eye when she was a little bit older, so perhaps they found it easy to think of her as a flawed specimen."

Flora flinches.

Lewis lets out a ragged sigh. "It was a tragedy, and we were in shock and grieving, but we could have survived it. We could have rebuilt our lives—but Flora wouldn't allow that to happen. She couldn't give us that chance."

"I couldn't live with them and pretend," she says. "How could I stay there, knowing what I'd done? I didn't deserve beautiful children and a husband who loved me. And I couldn't live a lie, no matter how much Lewis wanted me to. What I really wanted, *all* I wanted, was to die. I prayed it would happen, without me having to do anything."

"There were moments when I could have killed her," says Lewis. "Not because of Georgina—because she was proposing to leave me, when all I'd done was protect her and our family."

"So you left?" I ask Flora. "You abandoned them all?"

"That's exactly what she did," says Lewis. "And cut off all contact. With everyone. I had to go with her to tell her parents. She begged me to do the talking, and I did it. I fucking did it, Beth. Then I had to tell Thomas and Emily that she couldn't be part of their lives anymore. Flora and I came up with the least upsetting story we could think of in the circumstances: Georgina dying had caused her to have a breakdown, and now she wasn't herself anymore and couldn't be around anyone, including them. It was devastating for them to hear that, but what could I do? I could hardly say, 'Mummy'll be back any minute now, she's just nipped to the shops.' She wasn't ever coming back to us. She'd made that clear, and I could see it. Even sitting in a room with me, having the conversations we needed to have, she couldn't stand it. It was like she'd developed an allergy to all of us—me and the children."

"To myself," Flora corrects him. "You reminded me, that's all—of the difference between what I used to be and what I'd become. It was better for Thomas and Emily not to be around me, given the state I was in. Lewis was a good dad, Beth. *Is* a good dad. Any damage I did by abandoning the family, he repaired."

"I'm not going to deny that. Fuck it." Lewis shifts in his chair. "I'm not. We had a rough few years, but slowly, steadily,

Thomas and Emily—whose names Flora refuses to say, have you noticed, Beth?—grew into the happy, secure teenagers they are now. Thanks to me. And it has to stay that way. Over my dead body are they going to find out now, after all these years, that Georgina's death wasn't a tragic accident."

"I won't say anything," I tell him. What good would it do, at this late stage? "I'm so sorry. I can't imagine how awful it must have been."

"Well, what can I say?" Lewis laughs bitterly. "Thank you, Beth, for making this little trip down Memory Lane possible. Can I go now? I need to get back to the office."

"Without me?" Flora asks expressionlessly.

"Yes, without you," he snaps. "I'm going to take a little break from trying to help you, if that's okay."

"But how will I get back to the house?"

"You'll figure out a way." Lewis stands up.

"I've got more questions," I say.

"Oh, I bet you have. Flora can answer them." In an angry, singsong voice he says, "Flora has decided today is a talking day. Good-bye, Beth."

Without another word, he leaves the room.

22

I stand up and walk over to the window, to give Flora a chance to compose herself. She started to cry when Lewis left and hasn't stopped since. Sunlight is streaming into the room, streaking the carpet and furniture with stripes of gold. They create a bar-like effect and make me think of prison—something that was in my mind even before Lewis and Flora came up to my hotel room, thanks to Chimpy.

There's a darkness in here that's almost suffocating; the light from outside can't touch it. The shimmering turquoise swimming pool, palm trees and orange sun umbrellas on the other side of the glass look as implausible as a stage set that's way too good to be true.

I flick the catch, slide the balcony door open and step outside. The hot air hugs my face. It's a welcome relief. When the heat gets too much, I slide the door closed again.

"You should tell the truth, Flora. To your parents, the police, everybody. Instead of walking around like a shadow, hiding a horrible secret. You shouldn't have to live like this for the rest of your life."

"It's better than having everyone know. Don't tell me it isn't. You can't imagine how it feels to have done what I've done. It would destroy my parents if they knew."

"And Thomas and Emily?" I say, wondering if Lewis is right about her unwillingness to say their names.

"Them too. I don't want to hurt Lewis's children any more

than I already have. He's been good to me. No one deserves any more pain."

"Including you?"

"I deserve nothing," she says quietly. "Nothing good, anyway."

"They're your children too, Flora. Not only Lewis's."

"Not anymore."

"How much of what you've just told me do Kevin and Yanina know?"

"Nothing." An impatient look passes across her face. "Why do you think I married Kevin? If he'd known, I wouldn't have gone anywhere near him. After Georgina died, when I left everything behind, I thought I'd be alone forever. That was what I deserved and what I wanted. Then I met Kevin, and he . . . he pursued me. I realized that I could maybe have a family again. As long as no one in my new life knew the truth. I'd changed my name by then, to Jeanette Dawson. Dawson was my mum's maiden name. You won't be able to understand this, but . . . I convinced myself I was a different person."

"You didn't tell Kevin you'd been married before?"

"He knew about Lewis, but not that I'd had any children with him. I lied about that. When I was pregnant with . . ." She stops. Starts again. "I made sure he never came to doctor or hospital appointments. It wasn't hard. He had no interest in them. He's not interested in much, Kevin. I don't love him or particularly like him."

"Then why . . . ?"

"Can't you guess?" Flora smiles through her tears. "I wanted more children. Knowing you don't deserve something doesn't make you stop wanting it. I was weak. I shouldn't have let myself accept Kevin's proposal, but once I did, the rest just—" She breaks off and frowns. "No, it didn't just happen. That's not true. I let it happen. I was Jeanette now, so it was okay. That's what I told myself—that it would be okay."

"So you had two more children? With Kevin, not with Lewis?"

"They're Kevin's, Beth."

"You had two children, and you called them Thomas and Emily."

"You know I did. That's why you're here."

"Why did you choose those names?"

She stares at me. Is she hoping I'll withdraw the question?

"Why, Flora?"

"I don't know. I can't explain it. I wanted what I'd lost, I suppose. Kevin would have let me call them anything. Up to me, he said."

"How did he feel when you told him you were going to Florida suddenly? If he knows nothing about what happened in the past, how did you explain this trip? Isn't Kevin wondering what the hell's going on?"

"I blamed it on you," says Flora.

"Me?"

"When Lewis rang me to say you'd been in touch, my heart nearly stopped right then and there. I hadn't seen or heard from him in twelve years. I was a nervous wreck. There was no way you'd contact Lewis after so many years unless you suspected something—I knew that. And Marilyn Oxley, my neighbor . . . she'd told Kevin that you'd asked her if our children were called Thomas and Emily. I had to get away from you, Beth. To make sure *this* didn't happen. I didn't want you to know, and I knew I could so easily break down and tell you if we met. You were my best friend for so long. We knew everything about each other, didn't we?"

I nod.

"I couldn't risk that. Lewis knew it was a risk, too. He said, 'Cast iron rule: you don't see her, you don't speak to her, you don't let her come anywhere near you.' So I did everything he said, like I always have, apart from that one night—the night

Georgina died, when I wanted a drink and then another drink so badly that I ended up killing my own daughter."

"What happened to Georgina was an accident, Flora. If you want to say it was an accident that only happened because you made a bad decision, then tell yourself that . . . but even so, you should stop torturing yourself. Everyone makes bad decisions. And it was twelve years ago. Isn't it time you forgave yourself?"

"What an excellent idea." She eyes me coldly. "I'll just do that, then, shall I?"

"Has Lewis told you you should forgive yourself? If you always do what he says—"

"He said it when it first happened, before I told him I was leaving. Hasn't said it since." She smiles as if at a fond memory. "Lewis has always been extraordinarily selfish. Breathtakingly so, really. If I was going to remain as his wife and the mother of his children, then he didn't want me to torture myself. It would have a terrible effect on them—his family. But if I'm leaving? Well, then he's certainly not going to tell me to forgive myself, is he?"

"You said a minute ago that he'd been good to you."

"He has, purely for his and his children's sake. He doesn't care about me anymore. Couldn't you tell? I don't mind. I still appreciate his help. I'm as obedient an ex-wife as I was a wife." Flora laughs as if we're having an ordinary conversation. "When he rang to say you'd contacted him on Instagram, I followed his instructions to the letter: pretended we were still together and living in Florida, a happy family of five. Going along with his plans was my only option. He could think straight and I couldn't."

"And you told Kevin what? 'Someone I want to avoid is poking around in my business, so I'm going to have to go and stay with my ex-husband in Florida'?"

She recoils. "I'm not staying with Lewis and his children. I'd never do that. He wouldn't allow it, either. Lewis arranged another house for me to stay in. I'm not part of their life anymore, and we both want to keep it that way. I'm a coward, Beth. I'm not confident and brave like you."

"I asked about Kevin," I remind her.

"Kevin understood, yes. He doesn't pry into my business. That's one of his best qualities."

Got it. Prying is bad. Message delivered, loud and clear.

"So together, you and Lewis made a plan to mislead me because you thought the questions I was asking might lead to the truth coming out." As I say it, I try to imagine the conversations they must have had if this is true. I picture Kevin Cater, not privy to these discussions, saying to Yanina, "Flora and her ex-husband must have some unfinished business to deal with, relating to this old friend. I'm not going to pry."

"We knew you knew about the names," says Flora. "How could I explain to you why I'd used the same ones? I knew it was the first question you'd ask me if you got the chance. There's no explanation that makes any sense apart from the truth! And if I told you I was estranged from . . . from . . ." She covers her face with her hands.

"From your oldest two children," I say. "From Thomas and Emily Braid."

"If I told you that, you'd have asked why. You'd have demanded an answer. You remind me of Lewis sometimes, with your determination to get the result you want. I'm not a strong person, Beth. You'd have broken me down eventually. Lewis and I both knew that. We agreed that the best thing to do was get me out of the way, where you couldn't find me."

"Except I did."

"You did." Is that hatred in her eyes, or something else? "Here you are."

"And here *you* are, telling me the story. What if I go to the police now?"

"You promised Lewis you wouldn't tell anyone but Dom."

"Flora, Lewis might be your lord and master, but he's not mine. What if I break the promise I made?"

"You won't. You wouldn't do that to me, or to any of the other people who would suffer if you did. Georgina's been gone twelve years. What would it achieve to stir things up now? Have some compassion for Lewis, if you've got none for me."

"Flora, how can you say that? That's so far from—"

"He isn't my lord and master, but he is my savior," she talks over me. "He says he's not doing any of it for me, but I still get the benefits. He made this escape plan for me. He's helped in all kinds of ways—like letting me and Kevin have the Hemingford Abbots house, which he didn't have to do. It was still his, he hadn't sold it. And once he'd moved to America—"

"Flora, I know you're lying." The words spill out of me as a sudden realization hits hard. How did it take me so long to see it? "You're so intent on cutting all ties with your old life that you disown your kids, change your name, cut off your parents—something you'd never do, by the way—*and then you choose to live with your new husband and bring up your new children in the house where Georgina died?* You expect me to believe that?"

Flora stands up. "I don't have to talk to you," she says. "Not anymore. You already know the only thing I wanted to keep from you. Do what you want with it, I don't care."

"Really? That's not plausible either—that you suddenly don't care about the effect it would have on your parents, for example, if I were to go to them next week and tell them the truth."

Flora moves toward the door. I try to block her path, but she shoves me hard. I land on the bed on top of my bag.

told everyone that I'd found Georgina lifeless and smothered in the bed with Flora, who'd passed out from too much drink. I didn't say that. I protected my wife. I knew she wouldn't have survived a week in prison—and yes, I believe some mothers who recklessly endanger their newborns do end up behind bars, even if they cry and say it was an accident. So I told everybody that Flora wasn't to blame, that I came in and found Georgina in her cot. Blue, not breathing. I said nothing about the wine Flora had drunk."

"Flora *wasn't* to blame," I say. "You were."

Lewis frowns. "I know. Don't let terror turn you stupid, Beth. I didn't pin the blame on myself, obviously. My point is, I could have told the world that Flora killed Georgina, and I didn't. I spared her that ordeal and that shame—possibly a criminal record too. I did all that willingly, because I didn't want to be unnecessarily vindictive."

Flora makes a strangled noise.

"But for an offense so severe, there had to be a price," Lewis goes on. "Oh, wait—you think I'm talking about the killing of Georgina? No. Not that offense. Tell her, Flora."

"The offense was that I got pregnant when Lewis didn't want another baby," she says mechanically.

"Deliberately, Beth. That's not on. You won't admit it now, but you know it's something no decent person would do. Then she gave birth too early, to a cross-eyed creature that was certainly no part of the amazing family I wanted—the one I *had* until she ruined everything. Did Flora cause Georgina's death? Yes, in a way. Without her scheming, there'd have been no Georgina. No one would have needed to die. That would have been better for all of us—you too, Beth. Flora's lucky still to be a free woman."

Where should you be? HMP Peterborough.

"Anyway, we very much were where we were, at that point." Lewis shrugs. He stands up with a heavy sigh. "As I say, I offered Flora a solution to our predicament that I hoped would work for all of us. She was to detach herself, immediately, and disappear. I'd cover all expenses. Thomas, Emily and I would then be free of her taint, and Georgina's, and able to get on with the rest of our lives. We agreed that after she'd gone, I'd tell the children that she'd had a breakdown and couldn't face being part of our family anymore after what had happened to their sister. And that was that. Separate lives. That's how it would have gone, if I hadn't been too soft-hearted."

"You aren't soft-hearted." Flora steps forward. Her words spill out in a messy rush, barely distinct from one another. "You're the opposite. You say you didn't want to be vindictive, but you did. You still do. You want me to suffer as much as possible."

Lewis nods. His eyes flash, as if her disagreement has given him new energy. "Interesting interpretation, Mrs. Braid. I've not heard any of this before, Beth. Flora never talks back. I wouldn't allow it. Today's different, though. It's True-Feel Reveal Day here in Delray Beach, Florida!" He chuckles. "Go on, Flora, have your say. I'm sure you're not afraid of anything, are you?"

"What should I be scared of?" she says. "You're never going to kill me—you've got your playhouse on Wyddial Lane with all your toys in it and I'm the main one, aren't I? Without me to torture, you'd have no interest in playing your game, and you *love* your game. You're incapable of loving any human being properly, but you love the game, and the power it brings you."

"She calls it a game, Beth," says Lewis in a voice designed to sound sad. "I call it giving her another chance. I think we need someone more objective than either of us to be the judge—you, for instance. Sure, you're on Flora's side against me, but you've got a good brain. Did I do her a favor or am I the sadist she thinks I am? Tell her the story, Flora. Actually, wait."

Using his free hand, he pulls his phone out of his pocket and sets it down on the table. "I'm going to record this. It's good to have it all stored, for the official record. In case one day I write my story." He grins. "Who lives, who dies, who tells *your* story, Beth?"

His eyes flit up and down as he sets the phone to record. They're never off me or the gun in his hand for long enough to give me a chance.

"Recording," he says, looking at Flora. "On your marks, get set, go. Let's let Judge Beth decide."

"He said I had to go," Flora says in a dull voice. "Far away from all of them. Lose my family. He would pay for my new life, but it had to be somewhere where there was no danger I'd bump into any of them by chance. First he sent me to Scotland. Until the job opportunity here came up, and he made a different plan: to put me back in the house where he . . ." She chokes on the words. Starts again. "Where it happened. And keep me there. He'd keep an eye on me, he said, to check I was coping. He didn't care what happened to me, but he pretended to. That's what he does: pretends or uses the truth as it suits him, so that I never know what to expect. Him keeping tabs on me was a control thing. That was how the phone calls started. The Daily Responses."

"Beth won't know what those are," says Lewis wearily, as if Flora's a toddler who's testing his patience to the limit.

"She knows."

"And if you didn't go to Scotland, and then back to Wyddial Lane, if you didn't do his sick phone ritual every day, what did he say he'd do to you?" Hearing myself ask the question, I realize I'm not as scared as I was at first. I don't know why not. Lewis still has a gun pointed at me. Maybe burning hatred flowing through you for long enough makes you braver. "Did he threaten to tell Thomas and Emily that Georgina's death was your fault? That you'd been a bad mother and killed her?"

Flora nods. "My parents too. It would have destroyed them.

They'd have believed me over him if I'd told them everything, but I couldn't risk it because he'd threatened something far worse than exposing me as a killer, even if he hadn't stated the threat in words."

"If I didn't say it in words, Flora, how could I have made the threat?" asks Lewis.

"Innuendos, suggestions," says Flora. "You know how you did it, and I knew exactly what you meant: if I didn't keep my mouth shut and obey you, always, in every detail of what little life you'd left me, then you'd kill someone else I loved. Thomas and Emily, probably. Or my parents. Maybe all of them. There's nothing too evil for you, and you don't care about anyone apart from yourself."

"That's not true." Lewis looks angry. Insulted.

I watch his face carefully, not quite believing what I'm seeing.

"I cared about my family. You corrupted it beyond repair," he tells Flora.

"Even if you cared once, that changed," she says. "Your obsession with making me suffer took over. You got addicted to it at some point. I'm not sure when. Maybe when the Florida job prospect came up and you realized you could force me to live—" Flora stops with a strangled sob. "Live in *that* house again—the last place I'd ever want to go back to. The house where you killed Georgina, the house you make me live in."

"Who are Kevin Cater and Yanina?" I ask.

"Is that a trick question?" Lewis sneers. "They're Kevin Cater and Yanina. Yanina Milyukov. Kevin Cater used to work with me years ago, when we all still lived in Cambridge. Yanina's his girlfriend. I'm glad you brought them up." There's an edge of grim determination to his voice. "They're the people I pay to keep things running smoothly. Flora's not reliable these days, as you can see for yourself. She has two young children, whom she'd be incapable of looking after properly on her own. When

I say 'pay'—" He breaks off and laughs. "'Through the nose' is the only way to describe it. I pay Cater and Yanina a fortune, in fact. Not that I mind—they're worth it. Most people would ask awkward questions, or want a say in what happened in the house. Not them. They do as they're told."

"And they don't know the rest. They have no idea how much they're *not* told," says Flora. "I've always been too frightened to say anything. They don't know you're a murderer. They don't know that every time you pop back from Florida you . . . you . . . *I hate you!*" She screams at him, bending double as if someone's snapped her in half. "I wish you were dead, I wish *I* was dead," she sobs.

As if nothing has happened, Lewis says to me, "I pay Thomas and Emily Cater's school fees too. They're not cheap. I do all of this so that Flora can have a second chance. A new family."

"Pretending to be Kevin Cater's wife?" I say. "That's her second chance? While his girlfriend pretends to be the nanny?"

"Flora's a mess," Lewis says dismissively. "No one would have believed in her as the nanny. Plus, I wanted her to be able to play Mummy again. Yanina's got a Russian accent, as nannies often do. It worked better that way."

I look at Flora. "How could they go along with it?" I ask her. "Are they monsters too?"

She shakes her head slowly, woodenly. There's a puzzled look in her eyes, as if she's searching for the right word to describe Kevin and Yanina.

"You've never had a really large amount of money, have you, Beth?" Lewis says. "Life-changingly large, I mean. Cater and Yanina have. I've never explicitly told them that Flora's drunken binge caused Georgina's death, but I know it's what they both think happened." He looks pleased with himself. "Remember, Flora has also 'gone along with it,' as you put it. All these years. She could have walked away from that house any time she chose to. She could have gone to the police if she thought what I was inflicting on her was so terrible. But she never did, and she never will. That ought to tell you something."

"Because I know you'd kill my children," Flora tells him. Like an everyday wife reminding her husband of the bad thing that will happen if they don't both take care to avoid it. I know what I'm hearing, yet part of me is still thinking, "Is there anything else that this could all mean? It can't mean what I think it does."

"You're making that up." Lewis sneers at Flora. "I've never said it."

"Why are they called Thomas and Emily?" The gun in his hand is no longer pointed at me. I didn't notice him lowering his arm, which is now by his side. If he fired, the bullet would hit the floor.

"Who?" Lewis asks me. His face breaks into a grin. "*Think* about it," he says.

"Thomas and Emily Cater. I know they're both yours," I tell him.

"Of course they're mine." He looks impatient. "Who else's would they be?"

I wait.

"What more do you want to know?" Lewis asks. "I told you, I felt sorry for Flora. She'd deceived me and trashed my family, and I knew exactly what she deserved, but . . . I don't know. I hate to admit it, but maybe on some level I still loved her. I had Thomas and Emily, and she had no one. She was still my wife, still *mine*. I had to do something with her, I couldn't just leave her to rot. Then I realized there was absolutely no reason why she shouldn't have a second family." His face hardens. He stares at me, eyes wide, as he says slowly, "One. Baby. At. A time."

I stare back at him, full of a cold numbness. Is this what it feels like to look at the worst thing you've ever seen? I'm not really feeling anything, not anymore.

He says, "While Flora was pregnant—this time *with* my permission and without hers—it came to me. Of course the baby had to be called Thomas, if it was a boy. And a girl would be Emily. Same house, same names. Are you starting to understand, Beth? I saw a way of giving Flora some of it back, some of her old life. Me, from time to time. Every day, on the phone. A Thomas. An Emily." He walks toward Flora. "And one day soon, I hope, a Georgina," he says quietly. "We'll just have to keep trying, won't we?"

Any second now, if he keeps walking, he'll be facing away from me.

And you're going to do what? Run at him, try to overpower him? Risk getting killed sooner?

"I'm not lucky. I'm not lucky," Flora repeats as he walks toward her, her voice rising. "I'm *un*lucky."

"You're not as lucky as you could have been if you'd been more resourceful," Lewis says. "You could have made friends if you'd wanted to: mums at school, neighbors. You chose not to. It was your decision to become a virtual recluse, to sit around all day stewing in your misery."

"I'm not going to get pregnant again. I'm in my forties." Flora backs away from him as he approaches.

I stand completely still. How many chances to escape have I missed already? Do I have one now? This might be my one chance and I'm missing it because I'm thinking this instead of . . . I can't bring an alternative to mind. I'm frozen. Action feels impossible.

"Forties is nothing," says Lewis. "You're fit and healthy."

"Every time, I order my body not to get pregnant," Flora says. "Every single time."

Lewis laughs. "Well, it's ignored your orders twice already."

"You're a rapist," I tell him. "A rapist and a murderer."

"Everything you've done, you've done it to torture me," says

Flora as he moves closer to her. "Making me live in that house, making me have more children, calling them the same names." She's breathing hard and fast, as if she's been running. In my head, I'm running away from Lewis. I wonder if she is too.

"The lies you made me learn by heart to repeat to Beth, while my children that I haven't seen for *twelve years* are just around the corner, and I can't see them, not even once, for a second. What's next? Let's say you get your way and I have another baby—what's next on your torture list after that?"

"Why are you saying all this now?" Lewis asks her.

There's a pause. Flora looks at me. Then she says, "I don't know."

"Your friend's here, and you've got some moral support for the first time in years. Clearly it's gone to your head. But Beth's not going to be here for much longer. Maybe you aren't either. Did you stop to think of that?"

He's going to kill us both. And if he does that, if he's killed once and will happily kill twice more . . . "Why has Thomas been taken out of school?" I ask him as he raises his arm to point the gun at Flora's head.

Her eyes fill with fear. "What?" she says.

"Ignore her," says Lewis. "She's talking shit."

"I'm not. Thomas isn't at the school anymore. And Emily's place has been canceled. Kevin and Yanina . . ." The missing words stick in my throat.

What did Kevin and Yanina do? And why, if Lewis knows nothing about it? They're supposed to do what they're told in exchange for life-changing money.

"What the *fuck*?" Lewis swings around and points the gun at me. It makes a clicking noise. Everything inside me starts to shake. His face is twisted: a mixture of rage and confusion.

Flora lunges at him from behind. The gun falls from his hand and lands on the floor. He trips and tumbles, taking her with him. She lands half on top of him, with a noise that's halfway between a scream and a howl. Lewis lunges for the gun, not quickly enough. It's in my hand.

It's in my hand. I stare down at it.

Lewis lunges toward me.

"Beth!" Flora screams.

"Lewis, don't!" I say, aiming the words at his phone on the table. "Don't kill me. Please."

He was about to lunge again, but he stops. Confusion spreads across his face. He can't think why I'd say those words when I'm the one holding the gun. "Don't do it!" I cry out. There's nothing fake about the panic in my voice.

"What . . . ?" Lewis tries to scramble to his feet.

I fire the gun.

27

"Why did you turn it off?"

"You're not saying anything. No point me recording silence."

"I've already repeated it twice."

"I know. And I'm sorry to have to ask you to go through it again. You've been so incredibly helpful."

"Wasn't the recording on his phone clear enough for you?"

"Loud and clear, ma'am. You have no idea how grateful I am to have it. But I need to hear the story from you, in your own words. I know you've already told Detective Gessinger, but—"

"And then can I call my family?"

"Absolutely for sure. Don't worry, they know you're safe. I reached out to your husband myself."

"Can't we do this after I've phoned home? And slept? I've missed a whole night's sleep."

"I have an idea: how about if you only tell me about the last part, for now? Then tomorrow we can talk properly, once you're rested."

"Where's Flora?"

"Detective Gessinger's with her now. She's hanging in there. Her parents are on a plane, on their way over."

"And her children? She's got four children!"

"Mrs. Leeson, please let us take care of everything. There's nothing you need to concern yourself with. Trust me. We've got this."

"Okay."

"Now, I need you to tell me what happened. From the beginning."

"All right. I—"

"Wait a second. Resuming the interview at 1100 hours. Detective Sophia Steel interviewing Mrs. Elizabeth Leeson. All right, Mrs. Leeson, I need to hear your account of how Mr. Braid lost his life."

"He had a gun. He'd come to the house to kill me—he made that clear over and over again. Kept saying it. I don't know about Flora. I didn't think he was going to kill her—I think he might even have said he wasn't—but then later he implied that maybe he would. It's all in the recording, just listen to it."

"Go on. You're doing great."

"He would have done it. He'd have killed both of us. I had no idea that my question would throw him in the way it did. I assumed—"

"Wait, back up. You asked him a question while he was pointing the gun at you?"

"I think . . . I'm trying to remember. I think he was facing away from me, pointing the gun at Flora, when I asked him why Thomas had been taken out of school. I assumed he knew that had happened, but he didn't. He was shocked. We both saw it, me and Flora. Any second, he was going to kill us. We both knew it. When he turned around to say something to me, she ran at him and either grabbed him or shoved him, I don't know which."

"And then?"

"The gun fell out of his hand. Landed on the floor. Oh—he'd clicked it just before that happened, like people do when they're about to shoot."

"What happened after the gun fell?"

"I picked it up and started to back away toward the front door. I was thinking I could open it, run outside and scream for help. Lewis and Flora were both on the floor at that point. She'd landed on top of him. He was struggling to climb out from under her. Then he did, and he grabbed a knife from the block on the kitchen island. He started walking toward me, holding the knife like this—his hand was level with his head, in position to stab down."

"Go on. This is what we need. You're doing well."

"I was close to the door, and he was coming toward me slowly. I thought I'd have time to get out before he got to me, but the door was locked. He must have locked it when he first came in. I couldn't unlock it, not at the same time as keeping the gun on him, and if I didn't do that . . ."

"I understand."

"He was coming closer. I couldn't get away. There was no-where for me to go. I knew he was going to kill me if I didn't do something, so I aimed the gun at his right arm—or I thought I did. I never meant to hit his head."

"You've never fired a gun before?"

"No. Never."

"Then the odds were against you hitting him at all. How much distance would you say there was between you when you fired that shot?"

"I don't know. The closer he got, the more scared I was. I fired when I knew . . ."

"It's okay. Take your time."

"When I knew that if he came any nearer I'd freeze and it'd be too late. I remember thinking, 'Soon he'll be too close and there'll be no point.' I shouted at him not to do it, not to kill me—"

"Excuse the interruption. You were the one holding the gun, and Mr. Braid was not yet close enough to reach you, and *you* shouted 'Don't kill me'?"

"I told you: he was walking toward me with a knife. Holding it like this."

"But you had a gun. Wasn't he worried you'd kill him? I mean, that's what happened, yes? You killed him."

"No, he wasn't worried. He still totally believed he was going to walk away without a scratch after killing me and Flora. He didn't think I'd ever fire the gun. He thought I was too weak. So did I, until I did it."

"All right. Thank you, Mrs. Leeson. We'll let you have a little rest, maybe call your family in England. And then—I'm sorry, but it's necessary—you're going to need to go back a little further and talk me through all this from the very beginning. How it all started."

Epilogue

Four months later

The narrow road winds around and around, perilous zigzag corners all the way up the hill. Every so often we pass a large pile of rubbish, bagged in multicolored plastic sacks, that's been dumped by the side of the road and left to rot in the sun. There's a strike going on according to Dom. I don't know how he knows anything about the work disputes of Corfiot refuse collectors; I never got to find out. When he started to tell us, Ben and Zannah both groaned and put their earphones in, and he gave up with a sigh.

"How can there be any more turns?" he asks. "I mean . . . this is it. We're at the top. But I think I'm supposed to turn right again here. Didn't Flora's email say turn right at the Lavandula bar?"

"Yeah. We must be nearly . . . Look, there. There's a sign saying 'Villa Agathi,' with an arrow."

"Okay," Dom says in a low voice. He sounds as if he's readying himself for an ordeal.

"It'll be fine," I tell him.

"Will it?"

"Yes. The kids aren't worried." I adjust our rental car's rearview mirror and inspect each of them in turn. They're half asleep, undisturbed by the loud music that's pouring into their ears.

"What are you expecting to happen?" I ask Dom.

He shakes his head, keeping his eyes on the bumpy track ahead.

"We're not going to walk into an awful scene of pain and anguish. Is that what you're worried about?"

"I wouldn't say I'm worried, exactly."

"It'll be fine. They're on holiday."

"We're not, though. Are we?"

"Not in the same way, no."

"Not in any way. This doesn't feel like a holiday to me."

"It's a short visit. Who cares what we call it?"

"I just want to be prepared," Dom says. "I don't know. Maybe that's impossible."

I put my hand on his arm. "Relax. Flora could have invited us any time in the past few months, to her parents' house, but she invited us *here*. To a villa on the top of a hill in Corfu. I think that means she wanted us all to meet in good circumstances this time. Happy circumstances. I know that's what it means."

"It's not all of us, though, is it? Will that be mentioned?"

"I don't know." It's a good question. "Flora and I will probably talk about it at some point. You can avoid it if you want to. You'll be able to go off somewhere with Ben, maybe."

"I can handle a conversation about unpleasant things, Beth. It's not that I'm worried about."

"Then what?"

"I don't know. Awkwardness, I guess. Not knowing what's going to happen."

"Here's what'll happen. Flora's going to say hello and ask how we are, like a normal person. Thomas and Emily will probably be jumping around on a trampoline, or splashing in the pool. Flora's mum or dad will offer us a cup of tea."

"I want a beer," Dom says. "I'll need one."

"And it won't be awkward. Not for more than about two

seconds, anyway. Flora's doing okay, Dom. She says the kids are too. They're getting better, all of them."

"And the other Thomas and Emily, the older ones? Do we mention them at all, or just carry on as if they don't exist? It's not that I want to bring them up, but . . ."

"No. Definitely don't."

"It's so horrible for Flora."

I agree, but I say nothing. Even saying, "Yes, it's awful," would make a terrible situation feel worse somehow, by officially confirming its existence. Not that it can be denied or changed. Thomas and Emily Braid are living with Lewis's mother, who has relocated to Delray Beach, in the same home they lived in with Lewis. They won't see Flora. She's written to them several times and so have I. So has Detective Sophia Steel. They've been told the true story of Georgina's death and everything that happened between their parents before and after that, and they don't believe it. Lewis's mother doesn't either. Their version of events, the one they're determined to stick to though there's no evidence for it, is that Flora and I conspired to murder Lewis, who never did a single thing wrong in his life. The one and only time I spoke to Emily Braid on the phone, a month ago, she said, "Why should I believe the mother who abandoned me and Thomas and who killed my little sister? I know that's what happened—Dad told us when he thought we were old enough to know. And she never once tried to make contact in twelve years. And then you and she plotted to murder him and get away with it. You make me sick!" I was cut off before I could say anything in Flora's or my defense.

It's not true, Emily. The truth is that only I planned to murder your dad, during those few seconds that I had the gun in my hand, when I realized that I could. I planned it alone, with no help from Flora. I made up the lie about the knife and him coming at me with it in his hand, I said what I wanted Lewis's phone to record for the police to listen to later; I thought of all of it, the whole story and how it would play out, in those few seconds, while I clung to the gun with my trembling hands. All Flora did was corroborate.

Then I lied to Detective Steel. I didn't aim for Lewis's shoulder. I aimed for his head, and, even with my hand shaking violently, I must have aimed well. And maybe in a looser sense it was self-defense, but I'm never going to be able to think of it that way, knowing how much I wanted him dead, how deliberately I pointed the gun at the spot right between his eyes, willing the bullet through the air and into his warped brain.

And then I lied to Dom. And to Zannah and Ben. And I'll never know their opinion of what I really did, whether they would praise me and say, "I'd have done the same" or disapprove because I killed a man, deliberately, wanting him to die. Praying for it with every cell in my body, and feeling proud once it was done. That's the truth, Emily.

"Maybe they'll change their minds one day," Dom says as we pull up outside turquoise-painted gates with a white sign on them: "Villa Agathi." Flowers have been painted around the name. "If Kevin Cater and Yanina can overhear *one* conversation between Thomas and Emily and change their minds about everything after taking Lewis's money for years . . ."

"But how will Thomas and Emily Braid ever hear their younger siblings' account of the things the horrible man from America used to say to Mummy when he appeared? Even if they did, they might not change their minds. They're believing what they want and need to believe because they loved Lewis. They adored him."

I don't believe Kevin and Yanina truly changed their minds, but I don't want to say so. Not now. I can't prove it's a lie, and I couldn't bear to hear Dom stick up for them. I'll never believe that they suddenly realized, after being unaware for years, that they were involved in something appalling, and took immediate steps to get the children to safety. They must have known, and tolerated it. Then I turned up, and they saw that they'd failed to convince me there was no cause for concern. Lewis's instructions were becoming ever more alarming and bizarre—Yanina dressing in Flora's clothes, Flora having to be flown out to Florida without the children—and then a policeman turned up asking questions, and Kevin and Yanina's convenient, lucrative gig started to feel more risky.

Then, maybe, they overheard Thomas and Emily talking and discovered that Lewis's treatment of Flora was a little bit worse than even they'd imagined. But I can't believe they cared, at that point. If their worry for the children's safety was genuine, surely they'd have bundled Emily into the car, gone to fetch Thomas from school and gone straight to the police or social services.

There's something that doesn't convince me about them phoning the school and handing in formal notice, canceling Emily's place. There was no need for them to do it, and it feels staged to me. Performative. So that they could claim, later, that they feared reprisals from Lewis to such an extent that they made a decision to take the children and flee to a different part of the country—which was what they did. Even if you did plan to escape, why think about giving notice to a school? Why not just go? Flora thinks they probably wanted to be upfront and end the relationship there and then, so that there would be no phone calls or inquiries the next day when Thomas didn't turn up for registration in the morning. Perhaps that's true. Flora will never ask Kevin or Yanina about it, or speak to them ever again, so there's no way of knowing.

"Are we here?" Ben asks as Dom switches off the car's engine. He stretches. "I'm tired." Tired or not, he's out of the car in seconds; Dom too. It's an old family joke: when we all drive home from somewhere, Dom and Ben are usually inside the house and halfway through watching a football match by the time Zan and I drag ourselves out of the car.

I turn and prod her leg. Her eyes snap open. She blinks.

"We're here," I tell her. "Sorry to wake you."

"You didn't," she says, stuffing her phone and earphones into the bag on her lap. "I was thinking . . ."

"Come on, you two," Dom calls out.

"What?" I ask Zannah.

She looks hesitant, then decides to go for it.

"Maybe I could try talking to Thomas and Emily Braid. I think I could maybe . . . I don't know. I don't know what I could do, but I'd like to give it a go. I'm the same age as them."

"No," I say. "I don't want you involved."

"And yet look where I am." Zan nods toward the villa.

Damn. Why is she so good at winning arguments?

"They'd tell you horrible things about me, Zan. They'd call me a murderer. I don't want you to have to deal with that."

"I can deal with whatever they say, Mum. Seriously." Looking out of the window, she adds casually, "I could also deal with you being a murderer as long as you only ever have one victim and that victim is Lewis Braid."

Does she know? Is that possible, even though I haven't told her?

"Shall I try and contact them, then?" She smiles innocently at me.

She knows.

I've no idea how I feel about that. My daughter knows I lied. My daughter knows what I did in Florida.

"Thomas and Emily Braid?" I say, playing for time.

Zannah nods. "I won't mention it to Flora now, in case it doesn't work. I just . . . I reckon I could convince *anyone* that

327

having a mother is a great thing, not to be missed," she says solemnly.

"Okay. You can try, if you want to." My eyes prickle with tears. I blink them away.

"Er . . . hello?" Dom leans into the car. "Did we come here so that Ben and I could stare at a wall, or . . ."

As he's speaking, the villa's blue gates open and Flora appears, with Rosemary behind her. She waves at us. She's smiling.

ACKNOWLEDGMENTS

I am immensely grateful to the wonderful team at Hodder, especially Carolyn Mays—my dream editor and also, luckily for me, my real-life editor. Thanks to Peter Straus, the best agent in the world, and Matthew Turner, and all at Rogers, Coleridge & White. Thank you to my wonderful American publishers, William Morrow, and to my amazing film and TV agent, Will Peterson.

A huge thank you to Kate Jones and Faith Tilleray for all their practical help and support. Thank you to my family—Dan, Phoebe, Guy and Brewster, who get a thank you and a dedication this time. Thanks to Adele Geras and Chris Gribble for reading and commenting on an early version, and to Emily Winslow, whose editorial advice improved this novel immensely.

Special thanks to Chris Ferguson, from Twitter, who gave me some very useful information about youth divisions of football teams. Thank you to my Dream Author program members who are just the best in every way! And last but not least, thanks to all my readers who write and send lovely messages all the time. Knowing that you're eagerly awaiting the next book makes me want to write it even more.